Mogford's

By the same author
'The Hired Lad'

Mogford's Winning Ways

IAN CAMPBELL THOMSON

Drum Publishing

First published 1999

Published by Drum Publishing,
P.O. Box 199, Wallingford, OX10 9XR

ISBN 0 9534713 1 4

Typeset by Galleon Typesetting, Ipswich
Printed and bound in Great Britain by Biddles Ltd,
Guildford and King's Lynn

Contents

This is a West Country story.
It is a work of fiction but I hope it reflects
life as it was around 1970 in a rural community.

To my wife Renée who has worked
diligently on the production of this book
and to a few steep acres where our children
were brought up with fields and woods to
explore in safety and remembering the
people we met along the way.

1
The stranger

MOGFORD had seen him around the village for the past week, sometimes walking, pausing to admire some of the older cottages, nodding the time of day in passing, but never stopping to talk. Mogford was intrigued. This was an elderly man who did not appear old. His step was springy, his eyes keen, sharply observant. There was a spry carriage to his lean frame and there he was, his little dog by his feet, taking his ease on the one bench that the village cricket club provided for the comfort of spectators. He was enjoying the feel of spring sunshine and no doubt listening to the ribald comments emanating from the shed which served as a changing room as the lads padded up for some early season practice.

Mogford had come to inspect his sheep which grazed the outfield. Indeed with cricket in some form or another afoot he had herded them into a corner where they were confined by sheep netting.

He approached the stranger and beamed a smile. "I always shut the sheep away when the lads are playing; ever since the vicar fell over one of them when he was backing up to take a catch. He wasn't best pleased, nor was the sheep when the vicar got up and chased it round the field." Mogford chuckled at the memory. "Nice enough day, birds are all busy."

The stranger smiled briefly. "There's a territorial

robin making his presence felt in a bush over there, a blackbird in the tree behind us and some tree sparrows twittering somewhere. Are you interested in birds Mr Mogford?"

"Only the ones that make a nuisance of themselves," Mogford said. "You know my name."

"Everybody knows you Mr Mogford. You have that small farm at the end of a long lane. Your wife is called Martha; you have a son Luke who helps you on the farm. You are something of a negotiator."

"Most people would describe me as a dealer," said Mogford with a smile. "Market trading, house clearance, anything considered but always fair, or anyway, as fair as I can afford to be. What about you?"

"Oh, not much to tell. Having a break, staying at The Bull, retired, you know how it is."

Mogford reflected on this. Retirement was something that never crossed his mind. He had just passed his fiftieth birthday and as long as he could get himself to a market he would probably never retire. "But your work, you must miss it," he tried.

"Oh not really, when you've been retired as long as I have, it becomes unimportant."

Mogford was too diplomatic to ask a direct question which might force an answer, better by far to engage in general conversation and pick up clues.

A large man emerged from the shed and headed towards the heavy roller. A voice from inside was heard to say, "I might have room to get my sodding pads on now he's gone."

"That's Blackie," Mogford said. "Gets his title from the big black moustache. Makes cider, was once the village blacksmith."

The large man was straining on the roller and calling for help.

"Keeps wicket," informed Mogford. "Not much technique with the bat but if he should happen to make contact they usually have to buy a new ball."

A thin elderly man appeared from a large house and hurried towards the action.

"Vicar," said Mogford. "Cricket is his first calling, but he does rant and rave a bit on Sundays. His services can be quite lively. Was a fair cricketer in his day, I dare say."

A raggle taggle collection of individuals were straggling out of the shed to group around one wicket for batting, bowling and close in catching practice.

"Not a very impressive lot," suggested Mogford.

"Some are a bit elderly," agreed the stranger. "Even a bit infirm. One is limping and the pitch is hardly the Oval."

"You've been to the Oval then?" Mogford was still looking for an opening.

"Oh yes, as one does," said the man.

Someone hit an untidy swipe which went straight to the hands of the bowler.

"Well I must be off," said the stranger.

Mogford watched his retreating figure. He was aware that he had made little progress. The man had not even divulged his name. Mogford wondered why. A recognisable name? Well known? Famous or infamous? No, not infamous, possibly well known and he had seen him taking a long look at Primrose Cottage and it was standing empty. This was someone worthy of his attention. They would meet again. He would make sure of it.

* * *

Martha looked round her kitchen. It was pleasantly warm from the Aga, sitting snugly in the recess of the old open hearth. Harness brasses glistened. Martha was taller than Mogford, who was on the short side; she was elegant and handsome in her mid-forties. Happy in her rural life despite an urban background, sharp of tongue when this was called for, she was nonetheless at peace with her home, her family and the animals which needed her care.

This was reflected in her dark eyes and the soft lines of her face as she viewed her surroundings.

"I think it'll do, Hammy," she said, addressing herself to an elderly Basset hound stretched full length by the Aga.

Hammy moved his head slightly and swivelled a red rimmed eye in response, moving his tail in minimal acknowledgement. Hammy had reached a stage in his doggy life when sleep and conservation of energy rated a high priority.

"Mogford should be home soon," she went on.

Hammy signalled agreement.

"As for that Luke. 'Got business in town,' he said. Goodness knows what he's getting up to. Fallen among friends no doubt."

This was too much for Hammy, who got up stiffly, and clomped outside to relieve himself; a ploy he used when at a loss what to do. He did not therefore hear Martha's thoughts on Luke; slightly angry, but a touch worried as well.

"That boy should have been home hours ago. Can't think where he's got to."

Hammy plodding heavily back indoors, was in time to be used as a foil for Martha's final worry. "I'll have to tell Mogford about Miss Pringle. He might not be too pleased with the arrangement. Perhaps I'll leave it till morning. Yes that's what I'll do, I'll tell him in the morning."

Sensing that the conversation had reached its conclusion, Hammy allowed his drooping lids to close, stretched the length of his body as close to the Aga as possible and snuffled his way back into sleep.

Mogford was soon to arrive. Luke stole in much later.

2
Hundreds to do

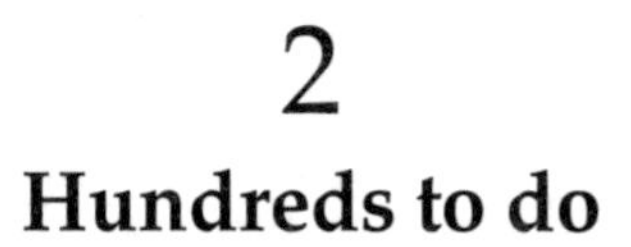

"I have hundreds to do," announced Mogford, and backed hurriedly into the yard. This figure of speech normally indicative of extreme industry, was sometimes used to terminate an argument, or escape from a difficult situation.

In this case he seemed to be conceding a lost cause. Martha appeared in the doorway arms akimbo. "And no tricks Mogford," was her parting shot. Martha tended to use only the surname except in times of extreme anger when she would append a 'Mr'.

Mogford retreated to confer with his pigs. Tricks eh! Hmm! Yes well, perhaps after all he had only lost the first round.

It had started when Martha had announced, after breakfast, that Miss Pringle – a young schoolteacher who had availed herself of bed and breakfast for two weeks in the summer – was coming for a short break before Christmas. Mogford had at first been pleased. All grist to the mill, he thought. He had been less pleased to learn that Miss Pringle had been invited as a friend. This was a principle Mogford was prepared to contest. Regular summer visitors, a good source of income, could become unprofitable friends. Besides, Martha could be match-making. Their son Luke although 25 years old and having for years been keeping a lot of 'maids' happy, had shown no signs of settling down. A good worker, despite a tendency to excesses in his private life, Luke's presence allowed his convivial father the freedom to visit markets to socialise and deal. A pretty London schoolmistress could pose a threat; she must be discouraged; Mogford had some thinking to do.

Miss Pringle had last stayed in July. It had been hot he remembered; she was tanned, and wore skimpy clothes, he was sure of that; glasses, a rather prim mouth; a bit flat perhaps, but pretty enough to cause the susceptible Luke some problems. In fact come to think of it they had spent some time together.

Come evening Mogford had taken a new tack. "Of course she must come m'dear, she'll be nice company for you." Martha, formidable in battle, but always quick to forgive, had gone to a lot of trouble with the evening meal, and the conversation had resumed over the roast pork.

"After all you are both teachers."

"Was," corrected Martha.

Mogford reflected briefly on that trip to Scotland for the 'Highland' which had resulted in their marriage. Indeed Luke had also been a result of that short visit.

Miss Pringle duly arrived. Mogford's heart sank. She was prettier than he had remembered, with smart town clothes and fair hair that bounced attractively on her collar. She wasn't wearing her glasses. Mogford was not unaware of the shortness of her skirt or her leggy slim shapeliness. He could see danger ahead where Luke was concerned. If only she would loosen up a bit she could be most attractive. Mogford knew about such things. The portents were not good.

In the kitchen Hammy struggled to his feet with difficulty, swung his head round slowly till the red rimmed eyes focused on Miss Pringle, gulped and slobbered, conferred a brief welcome with a stiff tail movement, and subsided again on the hearth rug. Even Hammy, short for Hamilton – Martha's choice – was showing approval.

Hammy had arrived on the scene about ten years ago,

having been part payment of a small debt. He was presented to Martha 'to keep you company m'dear' and Martha soon loved him dearly. For most of his life Hammy had listened attentively as Martha talked, fulfilling this role by fixing his eyes on Martha while cocking his head this way and that. His real understanding of vocabulary was limited to words concerning food and walks. A suspicion of such words would be signalled by a lift of the ears a short period of cogitation and an explosion of energy round the room.

During the last two years Hammy had aged dramatically, seldom went outdoors, and spent long periods asleep by the Aga. Here he resisted cajoling voices and prodding toes and was often used as a foot stool. Occasionally when the heat became unbearable he would move to a mat near the door to cool off. He suffered at one stage of his active life from gaseous abdominal rumblings and emissions which were unacceptable even to the indulgent Martha. He would sit up on such occasions and effect an abject look of apology. Hammy's pungency at such times could empty a room.

The vet was sure it was a dietary problem; extra mural scavenging was suspected. It transpired that Rip, the lean and over active farm dog, who spent all her spare time down rabbit holes, brought her prizes home for lardering. Hammy would 'vacuum' the area daily, find the buried spoils and gorge himself. The situation was supervised and certainly over the last two years Hammy's own sloth had guaranteed impeccable social credentials.

During the week Mogford worked assiduously at showing Miss Pringle life on the farm at its crudest. He would, he thought, tarnish any idyllic notions which might have lingered on from the summer holiday, a tactic which soon seemed doomed to failure. An attempt to sit at table in smelly clothes was routed by Martha. A discussion about the relationship between the fowl on the lunch table and the fine Maran cockerel perched on the windowsill elicited the remark, 'we must be practical Mr Mogford.' Connections between pork chops and runt pigs were stoutly refuted by Luke.

In fact Luke who could normally be relied on for the odd ribald remark or some slight vulgarity was behaving in the most decorous and exemplary fashion. Conversing quietly or listening intelligently he won an approving glance from Miss Pringle for the quote, 'we will never have communism, people are just not good enough,' when the far left of politics was being discussed. Mogford recognised one of his own favourite quotations. Luke had apparently given up belching, eating soup noisily and starting his pudding before everyone else. He held chairs and helped with the washing up. Mogford had not allowed in his strategy for this sheep's clothing.

Luke's self effacing good manners had the desired effect. On the third evening of Miss Pringle's stay she agreed to go out with him.

'Just a quiet drink,' he had said. 'In another village. Thatched roof, horse brasses, an inglenook – maybe a log fire. You'll like it. Goes back a couple of hundred years. You know, history.' He had thought it best to leave out the word romantic but he had it in mind.

'Sounds lovely,' she had said and meant it. Perhaps there was more to Luke than she had imagined. A feel for history – he was quieter, gentler than she remembered. When she'd been down in the summer he had seemed boisterous, more familiar, inclined to take liberties.

Miss Pringle lay on her bed and wiggled her bare toes. She had bathed and now, snuggled inside her cosy dressing gown she let her thoughts wander.

'We'll go about eight,' Luke had said. 'The locals will be drifting in about then. Gives the place a bit more colour.'

'A bit more colour,' Luke was full of surprises. She let her thoughts drift around him. He was tall with the build of an athlete, lean and supple. Dark crinkly hair. Handsome, she supposed, in a rugged sort of way.

With an effort she switched her thoughts from Luke and looked round her room. Martha had gone to a lot of trouble to make her feel at home. The same bright chintzy curtains she had had in the summer. The bed not too hard but not too soft either. The deep pile carpet could well have graced a stately home. Indeed it might have at some time; Miss Pringle was well aware of Mogford's dealing instincts.

It was all so different from her flat in Pimlico, so drab and shared with a colleague. And no view of any sort, just walls and chimney pots. She crossed to the window and looked out. A walled garden with a stream at the bottom. A wooden bridge giving access to fields rising beyond. Such a peaceful place with people happy with their lot. She wished she could feel more part of it, but she found it difficult. There were barriers, inhibitions, an innate shyness which she wished she could shed. Perhaps she could talk to Luke, this new gentler Luke. Now, what should she wear.

Squeezing into Luke's small van Miss Pringle felt light hearted and inclined to laughter. She knew she looked good in a tight black polo neck top and flared patterned skirt. The contact lenses troubled her sometimes but were worth the effort. She felt less of a schoolteacher without the glasses.

They bumped off up the lane. "You look chipper tonight," observed Luke. "And very smart if I'm allowed to say so."

Miss Pringle laughed outright and tugged at her sweater. "This old thing. I've had it all of three days."

"You do it justice," said Luke soberly. "And I'm going to call you Betty."

"Fine by me," Miss Pringle settled in her seat. She felt a little tingle go through her which she thought must be happiness.

The pub was all Luke had promised. The locals were trickling in and filling preferred seats. Some had personal pots hung in readiness. A fire blazed cheerfully. Luke was greeted on all sides and Miss Pringle's presence acknowledged respectfully.

"It's a real ale house," explained Luke. "Do you think you can handle it or shall I get you something else?"

"I'll give it a try. You choose, just a half though." Miss Pringle was enjoying herself and not unaware of appreciative glances from some of the younger patrons.

The noise level rose as some serious drinking got under way. Miss Pringle, not finding the ale to her liking slipped away from the exuberant group she was now part of and approached the bar.

She had just secured the attention of the landlord and asked for a glass of wine when she heard an enraged roar from somewhere in the room behind. She turned in time to see a large dishevelled man, obviously inebriated, charge across the room at the group she had left. Luke was laughing and calling something. She saw him grasp a table and overturn it in the path of the large man who crashed to the floor moaning with pain and rage.

Almost at once, as if a switch had been pressed, a fist fight broke out between the two rival groups. The locals sat around stoically, sipping, like ringsiders at a prize fight.

Miss Pringle could see Luke in the thick of it. He seemed to be revelling in it; then she felt a hand on her elbow. The landlord was holding the bar flap. "Best step this side m'dear, while I sort it out."

Miss Pringle watched from the relative safety of her new position as the landlord advanced into the room carrying a stout cudgel which he thumped loudly on the floor. "Stop or I'll have the law round. In any case I might break a few heads while I'm waiting."

The fracas stopped as suddenly as it had started.

"I'll work out the damage and share it out. Now, out," said the landlord. "Luke, I want a word. Get over to the young lady."

With the room back in some semblance of order the landlord came over. "Your car keys," he said. Luke handed them over. The landlord passed them to Miss Pringle.

"The lady had better drive. You've had a fair bit to drink. You'll have a bit to pay."

Luke tried to justify himself. "I know our cricket team was bottom last season. It was the way he said it . . ."

"Tell it to the lady on the way home," suggested the landlord. On the way home Luke slept. Miss Pringle had nothing to say. They parted without words at the foot of the stairs. Miss Pringle went up to bed sorely troubled.

* * *

The following evening with Miss Pringle due to leave in the morning, Mogford noticed something unusual. He was carving a fine piece of topside when he became aware of Hammy sitting up. The old dog had assumed the 'apology' position, head hanging, eyes swivelling, every wrinkle saying, 'I've done it, I'm sorry.' The atrocious smell soon rose to mingle with the aroma of roast beef and the reaction was instant and varied. Mogford for some reason was saying "good dog, good dog." Martha following an old familiar drill was opening windows. Luke catching a glimpse of Miss Pringle's expression forgot his veneer of refinement and filled the room with laughter. "That were a good un ole lad," he bellowed. He smacked Miss Pringle's bottom heartily as she passed on her way to the bathroom. She paused only long enough to administer a corrective slap.

Hammy his apologies made went back to sleep.

"Rabbits," ruminated Martha. "He must have got hold of some rabbits."

Miss Pringle left in the morning; she was wearing her glasses and her manner was prim. A hang-dog Luke put her case in the car. She thanked him coolly. Apparently having decided to establish a professional relationship, she insisted on paying for her room, at out of season rates, which she had calculated.

Mogford feeling Martha's eyes on him demurred then pocketed the money.

* * *

"Something's happened between her and Luke. That boy has put his foot in it, no mistake." Martha was holding forth over a cup of tea. "As for that old dog. It's years since he had a rabbit. At his age he couldn't catch a rabbit if it was sitting on the hearth rug. He hasn't been out; I don't see . . ."

Ill at ease Mogford was looking out of the window.

Luke restored to his normal roistering self could be heard giving maximum volume to a rugby song as he worked.

Someone passed the window pushing a bike. The handlebars were hung with rabbits.

Hammy cocked an eyebrow at Mogford and gave a muted 'woof'.

Mogford rose from the table, neatly side-stepped the dog and was gone.

Martha, hands on hips, stood in the doorway, the poacher fully in her sights.

He, well aware that the next ten minutes would not be pleasant, was topping up his inebriation with a hornful of 'home brewed'.

Martha's voice rang out clear and frosty. "Mogford come back here."

His voice drifted back. "Got hundreds to do."

* * *

The days were stretching out and there was a hint of sunshine outside. Indeed it was warm enough for Hammy to venture out for a little stroll.

Martha was taking a well earned breather rocking gently in the rocking chair and thinking her thoughts.

There would be grass soon. Maybe she should remind

Mogford that they needed a house cow. The last one had gone off barren six months ago. It was such a nuisance for Luke to have to fetch the milk. He wasn't over reliable either. Anyway she had been fond of the old cow. It would come to the window for a chat. She had missed it dreadfully. Yes! She would have a word with Mogford.

3

A calculated risk

"GAMBLING is gambling," stated Martha firmly.

"And I say," said Mogford "that there is a difference between gambling, which is a disease, and taking a calculated risk, which has more to do with earning a living." Mogford felt he had to defend his position as a sometime dealer.

At this Martha snorted and got up to clear away the breakfast dishes.

It had started as a discussion about Percy Percival's impecunious situation, brought about largely by the ownership of horses and a tendency for Percy to back them.

Percy's family had been 'gentry', and somehow even in his shabby clothes Percy had an air about him. Taxation and alcohol had got rid of the big house and most of the land in his father's time. Percy had inherited a small farm. The word was that he was 'behind' and could well lose the farm.

Recently he had met the gorgeous daughter of one of Mogford's cronies. They had fallen hopelessly in love, and in no time at all, they were married. Martha was sure Belinda would be good for him. Cynics said he was too far gone; once a gambler always a gambler.

To Mogford, Percy was now almost family, and as such, should be helped.

Martha turned from the sink. "Talking of money

Mogford, would we have enough in the bank to buy a good house cow?"

"A cow?" said Mogford. "That's a lot of money."

"You're not answering my question Mogford; at the bank; are we level?"

"Not really," said Mogford.

"Above?"

"No, not exactly."

"Below?"

"A little."

"Then I shall have to wait a bit," said Martha matter of factly.

It was Luke who got the word that Percy had bought a horse to go to the point-to-point. Luke with a tendency towards the dramatic, and with a vocabulary embellished with popular jargon had heard he was 'going for bust'. In other words, as he patiently explained, the Percival debt would be cleared if the horse won; if it lost . . . Luke drew a finger across his throat.

Mogford heard the same story from others. Martha, on the other hand, heard from Belinda that Percy had promised to give up gambling.

Mogford knew nothing of horses. Truth to tell he was more than a little scared of them. They were so big, so unpredictable.

He kept his eyes open and his ear to the ground; he was listening to 'form'.

The only serious opposition was from a big grey gelding, owned by 'old man Ryan', an Irishman, and a proper racing man by all accounts. A large land owner, and reputedly wealthy.

Mogford telephoned Percy, ostensibly to congratulate him on buying the horse, and discussed his prospects of winning.

Percy thought he had bought a splendid little mare; not too expensive; first class jumper; neat and fast, but he thought the straight gallop up the hill might favour a more powerful horse; Ryan's gelding for instance. Of one thing he was certain; if she was in the lead at the top, the downhill twists and turns would favour his mare.

With flat land hard to come by, the elliptical course had a distinct tilt, which meant that the horses started on the flat, galloped round a bend uphill to the halfway point, after which it was downhill all the way. After an initial jump there were no further barriers on the uphill, but to compensate, and to add distance, the downhill snaked to and fro, and jumps were frequent.

On the morning of the point-to-point, Mogford said to Luke, "We're going to the races today." Luke, no aficionado of the sport, but sure there would be a beer tent, agreed with alacrity.

"I'll just go up and get changed a minute," said Mogford.

When he came down, Luke whistled. "What a dude," he chortled.

"You look like Mountfield," commented Martha. Mountfield was the Vet.

"No matter," said Mogford, taking it all in his stride, "I dress for the occasion."

The pork pie hat had been replaced by a kangol cap, an extremely well cut tweed jacket (part of a job lot at a house clearance), buff waistcoat, cords, and his comfortable brown boots. A stout hazel walking stick replaced the more usual thumb stick.

"Have a good day," said Martha as they left, "and no gambling."

* * *

Mogford walked gingerly among the horses. A large prancing grey gelding, ears pricked, nostrils flaring, swung towards him. Instinctively he raised his stick and an explosive 'Huh' escaped him. The horse recoiled and resumed its dancing on the spot.

"Nothing wrong with his wind guv," a voice hailed him.

Mogford looked up at the little man resplendent in white breeches and striped silks, perched so high above him. "Oh ... ah ... well you never know," he said, feeling his way.

"You're a vet ain't you," the little man, obviously an ex-professional was ready to chat. "I can spot you chaps a mile off."

Mogford was quite unaware that in his panic he had inadvertently gone through the motions of a veterinary test for broken wind. He decided to play along. "No such thing," he denied firmly, and screwing up all his courage, approached the horse. He ran a terrified hand down the horse's front leg. "Expecting to win?" he asked.

"Of course," replied the little man, whom Mogford already thought of as 'the weasel', on account of his narrow build and tiny black eyes. "I have the best horse, I know how to ride."

Mogford stepped back shaking his head. "I shouldn't put money on it if I were you."

"Nothing wrong with the horse is there?" There was a note of anxiety in the weasel's voice.

"Not a thing," said Mogford with a mysterious little smile, "not a thing."

"Look here," said weasel, "if there is anything wrong I want to know."

Mogford kept his eyes pointedly on the fore leg and beckoned to Luke. "Run your hand down that leg and let me know what you feel."

"Nothing," said Luke, doing as he was bid.

"There you are," said Mogford, "nothing to worry about."

"But he's just a learner," squeaked the weasel. "Look here, if there is anything wrong I want to know."

"Nothing at all wrong, nothing at all, but tell me, has he stumbled at all on that leg?"

"Yes, yes," said weasel, "I had to pull his head up when we were warming up over there."

Mogford looked at the area indicated, rough with molehills and tufted grass, and thought perhaps all the horses had missed their footing at least once. He stood looking grave and nodding his head.

"I can give you some advice," he paused, "as a layman you understand."

"Of course, I understand," replied the little man.

"I would give him an easy ride up the hill, nurse him a bit, then let him go for it from the turn." Mogford could see that Luke was about to speak. Knowing Luke's tendency to over play, Mogford grabbed him by the shoulder and marched him off.

While still within earshot, he leaned towards Luke and in a stage whisper uttered the only veterinary word linked to horses he knew. "Bone spavin," he said without having the slightest idea what it meant.

As they neared the beer tent, Mogford stopped. "Got some business," he said. "Get the drinks in," and he scuttled off through the crowd.

* * *

The big moment arrived. The horses were under starter's orders for the Hunt Cup. The big grey was clear favourite, but late money had shortened the odds on Percy's horse. They were off. Experienced punters could see that the ex-professional was nursing the grey up the hill; holding a bit in hand. Percy was riding as if his very life depended on it. The mare reached the turn two lengths up and stretched into the downhill gallop. Wheeling into the turns like a cattle pony, jumping flawlessly, the mare held her two lengths advantage over the longer striding gelding, and ran out a clear winner.

About half an hour after the race, Mogford saw Percy and Belinda strolling arm in arm. Percy was still in his riding gear, his fair hair tumbling, a smile playing around his finely chiselled features. Mogford was reminded of sporting young gentlemen of another age. Every inch a

Corinthian, he thought. Belinda looked radiant. Indeed they seemed to be enveloped in an aura of happiness; not a care in the world.

He held out his hand as they approached. "Marvellous ride Percy," he said. "I expect you punished the bookies?"

"Not a penny old chap, hadn't you heard? I've given up gambling; mug's game; anyway, I'm a family man now."

"But the farm," said Mogford weakly.

"Oh that's all taken care of, not a problem."

They strolled on, eyes only for each other.

Later, Luke, with contacts in many local pubs, was able to fill in the details. Apparently 'old Ryan' had been so impressed, not only with the mare, but also with Percy's horsemanship, that he bought the mare – the figure was not disclosed, but rumour had it that Ryan had put Percy on his feet again – and had given him two or three horses to train for him. Belinda was pregnant.

* * *

"Like a fairy story," said Martha. "Just the sort of thing I like to hear with my morning coffee, don't you Mogford?"

"Oh yes," Mogford was glancing at his watch and listening.

"What's that?" asked Luke, "a lorry?" He went out.

Presently his face appeared at the kitchen window; beside him another face appeared. "Her name's Daisy," he bellowed through the window.

"Mogford," exclaimed Martha, "wherever did you get the money to buy that lovely Jersey cow?"

Daisy was looking at Martha and Martha was looking at Daisy. Mogford could see it was a love match from the word go.

Luke was tapping on the glass. "I think he had a bet on Percy's horse."

"Mogford," said Martha sternly. "You haven't been gambling?"

"Not really gambling m'dear," said Mogford. "Look at

it this way. I put on just enough to buy the cow if I won; when the odds were long at that; a fairly small investment; just a bit of business. No difference from doing a bit of trading in the market, come to think of it."

Luke had his nose pressed against the pane. "Gambling," he shouted.

Martha looked at her son, his nose comically distorted above a wide grin. Beside him Daisy looked back at her with placid undemanding eyes. A lot of good things had happened. The young Percivals were out of trouble and happy. Their baby was on the way. Mogford had in his own way, overcome financial constraints to produce Daisy out of the hat. No, he was not a gambling man.

She spoke to Luke through the glass. "Not gambling. I think you have to learn the difference between gambling and doing a bit of business, you could call it . . ."

Luke cut in, his grin widening, "A calculated risk?"

Mogford's eyes twinkled as he watched the cameo before him. Martha, so happy, Luke pleased for his mother's sake and perhaps a little proud of his father and Daisy now part of their extended animal family.

Martha said, "Best show Daisy round a bit, then let her stand in the cowshed. I shall want to get to know her. First I want a word with your father."

Daisy moved from the window with Luke clucking and encouraging, and Martha came to take Mogford in her arms.

"You're a good sort Mogford, in your way, most of the time – I am going to kiss you."

Presently Mogford said, "I enjoyed that. But do we need to stop there . . .?"

Martha looked at him severely, "It's not yet eleven in the morning and there's work waiting. But there – I could tell Luke to take Daisy to the far field. That would keep him out of the way long enough."

Mogford heard her call out instructions and Luke reply. "Maybe Da' would like to take her?"

There was a short silence, then he heard, "He's just taken his boots off. He's going upstairs for a bit of a rest."

* * *

In a remarkably short space of time Daisy had fallen into the routine of her predecessor. After morning milking she would find her own way through the ever open gate of the shady orchard where she grazed, to eat her fill, after which she would lie down to chew her cud. About four in the afternoon the tightness of her udder would send her home to remind Martha of her duties.

Martha had been baking, and was at the sink washing up her utensils one day in late spring, when Daisy appeared at the window, gently mooing her need to be milked. How fine she looked thought Martha; losing her winter coat already with the sleek summer version showing here and there.

"I'll just finish these dishes a minute," she informed Daisy. "Be with you in a jiffy."

Hammy on station as usual looked up briefly to make sure he wasn't being addressed and with what sounded like a sigh of relief settled down again.

"I'm just a bit worried about Chooky," Martha resumed her conversation with Daisy. "She's going broody again; we had enough fuss last time, only, I had her sitting on eggs before Mogford found out. It's all Luke's fault; that awful battery; he buys his chicks as day olds now; no need for broody hens; well it's not your concern, I suppose you want to be milked?"

Daisy mooed gently on cue.

"Well, I shall have to think of something. I can hear Mogford now. 'That old hen's broody again,' that's what he'll say."

There was a more insistent note in Daisy's next moo. Martha collected her bucket and stool.

4

Chooky's golden egg

MOGFORD was standing on the doorstep brushing his brown market boots when Chooky stalked jerkily past. Her body was crouched close to the ground, feathers ruffled with irritation, her cluck querulous. "The old hen's broody again," called Mogford.

Martha, busy with breakfast and well aware which old hen was under scrutiny, chose not to hear. "Your eggs are done, come and have your breakfast," was her response.

Mogford came in, his boots, with a market day shine, in his hand. "She's got to go this time," he declared firmly.

Martha merely tightened her lips. "Get your breakfast and be off," she suggested. "I have a busy day ahead of me."

Mogford could see he was on a sticky wicket. "But she hasn't laid an egg for years," he said.

"Perhaps you are forgetting all the chicks she has reared for you." Martha was responding now.

"But," tried Mogford again, "she doesn't lay, and of course, now we have the battery, and buy day olds, we don't need broody hens."

"I think she lays away." Martha was feeling cornered and had become tight lipped again.

Mogford saw just the chink of a compromise. "Well m'dear," he said smiling brightly, "let's find out, let's put her in the battery. If she lays within two weeks and lays regular after that, she stays; no eggs, out she goes. A deal?"

Martha seeing no immediate solution and needing to buy some time said, "deal," and they smacked palms in the time honoured way.

The cage battery had arrived more by accident than design. 'Cheap at the price' at a dispersal sale, Mogford had plans for a quick re-sale but son Luke had such enthusiasm for introducing the system, and made such a good presentation of the likely profit, that Mogford had fallen in with the plan.

Mogford was a little concerned sometimes by Luke's sudden short lived enthusiasms. This had started when he had joined the Young Farmers' Club. 'To improve my mind' was how Luke had put it. Mogford couldn't but agree that there was a need in this direction, but sometimes he suspected that Luke's frequent attendance at YFC events had something to do with the way the male/female membership ratio had recently swung in favour of the latter. Sure of the connection but uncertain as to whether a group of young females had flocked to the colours following Luke's enlistment, or whether Luke had calculated the odds before deciding he was needed, Mogford had no way of telling. He hoped the phase would pass.

Luke's enthusiasm had however in this instance, lasted long enough for him to insulate a building, erect the hundred cages, and invent the 'Luke' dimmer switch. This 'Heath Robinson' contraption was born of Mogford's flat refusal to invest in a time clock to bring the lights on at 2am. Luke had learned all about the pituitary gland, light intensity, and the importance of the extended working day. Mogford's solution was simple, switch off the lights at 10pm. Luke wanted a gradual fade out of light; after all 'how would Mogford like to find his way to bed in the dark.' Mogford said, 'he would have no trouble if he lived and slept in a cage, and anyway, he (Luke) seemed to manage quite well, often at two in the morning.' The upshot was that Mogford stood firm; he would not capitalise the project further. No time clock and no dimmer.

Necessity being the mother of invention, Luke set to work. The basis of the design was a plank on a pivot much like a see-saw. On one end was fixed an empty biscuit tin and from this end a length of fishing line threading its way through various eyelets operated another biscuit tin hinged to the metal lamp shade on one side. The other side slightly weighted was raised by the line in step with the movement of the see-saw. The power pack was a measured amount of water contained above the see saw, with a tap set to drip into the biscuit tin. The theory was that Luke could set the drip, go out for the evening, and forget about lights out. After hours of calibration and much adjustment, it worked, vulnerable only to plank walking cats and rodents. Having scaled this peak, Luke soon lost interest in the 'day to day' and a routine evolved in which Martha fed in the morning and Mogford collected the eggs in the late afternoon.

For two weeks Chooky sat sullenly in her cage. No eggs were forthcoming.

"Tomorrow," announced Mogford, remembering all the times in the past he had been pecked opening the coop door. Amazingly Martha had been able to do anything with Chooky in her broody coop days. Reach under to feel the eggs; lift the old lady off to feed. They would cluck to each other while Martha fed her tit bits; a pinch of cayenne pepper in the mash on cold mornings; the chill taken off the drinking water; Chooky lived a life of privilege. If Mogford came within feet, Chooky became a virago.

It was 'D' day. Mogford felt just a twinge of sadness. Chooky was a very fine specimen of the Wyandotte breed. She had to be at least three and a half years old, having broodied her way through three laying seasons.

"Well m'dear," said Mogford heavily, "we had better take a look."

Together they entered the battery house, and, wonder of wonders, there it was. Mogford rushed forward. "She's done it, the old devil." He reached to pick up the egg and in his excitement got within range of Chooky's sledge hammer beak. Unable to sit on the egg Chooky could at least defend it.

Martha approached, clucking softly, and collected the egg. The hen language continued and finally Martha said, "Same again tomorrow," and turned away.

"I must be going mazed," exploded a bewildered Mogford, "that old hen hasn't laid more than a dozen eggs in her whole life."

"Must be the battery," said Martha briefly.

The next day Chooky had laid again, and the next, then she missed a day and so it went on. About two days later she missed two days and Mogford thought the bubble had burst. But the day after, she delivered two eggs, and so the pattern was set, an egg most days followed by a lapse, redeemed by a double. This highly satisfactory state of affairs lasted some further two months until one afternoon Mogford came into the kitchen wearing a look halfway between incredulity and suspicion. "I have heard about the goose that laid the golden egg," he said.

"Yes," said Martha busy at the sink.

"I never believed that one even as a child," went on Mogford.

"Oh yes," Martha was still only half listening.

"But three eggs from that old girl in one day takes bit of swallowing."

The effect on Martha was dramatic. She crumpled into a chair and buried her face in her hands. "Three," she said, "she must have laid one. Oh Mogford," she said sadly, "I'm glad you found out. I couldn't have lived with it much longer." It all poured out; the whole subterfuge; the battle with the Presbyterian conscience; the end justifying the means. Martha had been taking eggs from the previous day's collection to compensate for Chooky's nil production: always correct as to colour and size, following the laying pattern of the other hens.

As the plot unfolded, Mogford could only admire the thoroughness of the 'save Chooky campaign'. However, he was well aware how much pain and soul searching Martha had lived with these past weeks. "So," Martha ended, "Chooky must go, and I'm sorry Mogford that I had to deceive you."

* * *

During the weeks that followed Martha threw herself into her work with redoubled energy. She believed in the 'hair shirt' method of absolving sin and every time she passed the empty battery cage she was reminded of her fall from grace.

She did notice that Mogford and Luke were spending time together. The conversation would change direction if she approached. They're up to something, thought Martha.

It was market day and Mogford was putting a final shine on his boots with a velvet pad. Martha was busy about his breakfast.

"M'dear," said Mogford quietly. "I have something to show you."

Martha demurred, "But your breakfast . . ."

Mogford had his boots on and was already making for the door, so Martha followed.

Round the end of the house, and there was Chooky's old coop.

"I always meant to do something about that door," grumbled Mogford. The door was a single piece of wood, located at the bottom and held with a turnbuckle at the top. A finger hole had been drilled to help remove the door.

Mogford inserted his finger. There was a loud squawk followed immediately by a yell from Mogford as he shot backwards, the door still attached to his lacerated finger.

But Martha was hunkered down, clucking and stroking. "Oh Mogford," she said, "you are a sly one."

Mogford accepted the compliment and stood sucking his bruised finger while Martha slid her hand under Chooky. The eggs felt smaller than hen eggs, she brought one out; khaki.

"Pheasants," she exclaimed.

"Yes, you see Luke had this idea . . ."

"Pheasants," snorted Martha again. "We're having no pheasants here." Then Martha looked at Chooky, lovingly tucking her alien egg beneath her feathers, and she looked again at Mogford hovering anxiously. Her face softened. "Well, perhaps we are."

* * *

Martha was always concerned that newcomers to the village should feel welcome. At the moment she was particularly concerned about an elderly gentleman who had moved into Primrose Cottage. He must be lonely, she thought. Just him and his little terrier.

She nagged Mogford about it. "Invite him for supper one evening," she said.

"It's not as easy as that," reasoned Mogford. "He's a very private person. Seems to value his solitude."

Martha valued *her* privacy. She was pleased to live in such a favoured spot. Set in a hollow with a stream rippling by, the front of the house looked south, and the back had a view of bluebell woods, parted by the farm lane leading up to the village. It was comforting to think that at the end of the lane was a community of people to which she actively belonged. Well there was always something going on in the village. Everyone was talking about the forthcoming cricket match. She was glad Luke was involved. It was 'healthy' for him; but she was getting a little tired of cricket talk.

She would rather someone did something about the old gentleman in Primrose Cottage.

5
The match

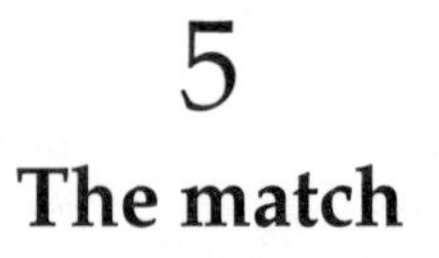

"A nice blend of youth and experience, that's what you want," said Mogford.

Luke stared at his father in amazement. "What I have, is an average age of just over sixty, and that includes myself and a schoolboy; and I'm still short of a man."

"Ah!" said Mogford, "I just happen to know of someone. The gentleman who moved into Primrose Cottage."

Luke nearly exploded. "But he must be seventy . . ."

"Seventy two," corrected Mogford, "and there's nobody else."

"You will ask him Luke," appealed Martha, "apart from anything else, somebody ought to introduce him to village life. Mogford will see to it." With that she got up from the table and bustled about clearing away the remnants of supper.

Luke still protested. "But he isn't even interested in cricket, if he comes to a match he only stays about five minutes, always writing by all accounts," but he had already capitulated, there *was* nobody else.

Luke was taking his responsibilities seriously. The cricket match, so much on his mind, was the annual end of season game between those who lived north of the pub, and those to the south. The pub was central in the one street village, and the catchment area took in the odd farm and a few isolated cottages beyond either end. Luke had been elected captain of the 'south' or as most people called it, 'below the pub' team, more for his social assets than any great cricketing ability. Unfortunately the split had left Luke with only four of the regular team; himself, a schoolboy who could bowl fast and straight; the vicar who bowled a good length and could turn the ball, but mostly from memory – he was bordering on elderly, irascible, and his sight was going and Blackie the regular wicket keeper.

Mogford had an aversion to all games played with a hard ball. His point blank refusal to take part unless they played with a tennis ball had not been helpful to Luke. However, Luke knew that Mogford was a keen student of the professional game, and in the morning he sought him out to discuss tactics.

They were agreed that they had the bowlers and the only wicket keeper. The 'above' the pub had the batsmen. Mogford gave a brief rundown on the batting abilities of the active members of Luke's side. The schoolboy although demoniac as a bowler, had many of Mogford's feelings about the hard ball. He would probably shut his eyes and get out quickly. The vicar would go to the first on-line ball, on account of his sight. Blackie would get a mighty six or nothing. Luke on a good day might get ten. From the geriatric tail, Mogford supposed, about six runs, while the opposition he thought, might notch up at least forty. The old gentleman from Primrose Cottage had not apparently come into his reckoning.

Mogford was often on the cricket ground. Not that he attended practices or pulled the heavy roller. He did however rent the grass keep, and kept enough ewes up there to keep the outfield tidy. It was here that he had on occasion encountered the 'stranger' as many people called the 'incomer' from Primrose Cottage.

He would be walking his diminutive Yorkshire terrier Fred, and obviously deriving pleasure from looking at the trees, the bird life, and Mogford's sheep.

Mogford had learned eventually that his name was Bob and he was indeed something of a scribbler. Mogford would have described him as of medium height, slim build, with a spring in his step that belied his years, and he had a very keen eye.

One day as they sat on the bench together, discussing sheep and the weather, a buzzard called high above. Bob had located the bird instantly. He admitted to having a pair of 'readers'.

It took all of Mogford's powers of persuasion to get Bob to agree to play. He indeed seemed to be a very private man to the point of shyness. It was only after Mogford had pointed out how important this festival game was to some of the old men – many, ex-players themselves, who would have turned out every year since the competition was first conceived thirty years ago – that he agreed to fill the last place.

Mogford went on to explain how rudderless the club was since the death of its president and benefactor, and how important cricket was to village life.

Mogford was a believer in the importance of tradition and symbols of village life, like the cricket club, and was distressed that so many young folk had to leave the community to find work.

* * *

Match day arrived. The sun shone, and there was a festive air around the field. Mogford's sheep had been penned behind some wire netting, and were looking on with interest.

There was much joshing and many reminiscences, and then it was time for the toss. Luke won and put the others in. The vicar was in devilish form; his in swingers helped by the condition of the wicket, and the odd sheep turd, were playing havoc. The wickets were falling. A spell of fiendish schoolboy fast bowling, again bouncing unpredictably, or skidding off a slippery surface, took more wickets. The fielders although in many cases rooted in immobility had nevertheless not lost the art of holding a catch, if one should come their way. Blackie despite his weight showed good footwork and presented a daunting spectacle to the batsmen.

'Above' the pub were all out for forty five.

Luke elected to open the innings with Blackie. Blackie was originally so named because he had been the brawny village blacksmith. Later generations had attributed his nickname to the heavy black walrus moustache. His face wore the roseate glow of one who makes his own cider. His enormous belly probably had something to do with living two doors down from the pub. Still the regular team wicket keeper despite his fifty five years and overweight condition, batting was not his strong point.

Luke got an accidental edge and ran a single. Blackie took the bowling and strode up the pitch to belt a short delivery into the next parish; instead he lost his footing on something soft, and landed on his back, where he lay like an upended sheep.

A leisurely stumping followed, and the vicar strode on wearing a single pad. He collected an l.b.w. on the unprotected shin and staggered back through the wicket, his lips moving.

"Careful," shouted Luke, looking skywards, "he may be able to lip read."

"L.b.w.," intoned the umpire, "among other things!"

The vicar limped off planning a sermon on forbearance and fortitude.

The stranger was walking on. His whites were immaculate. He was properly padded up and he wore a cap. He stood for a long time, bat tucked under his arm, looking up the wicket, then he took centre and was ready.

The first two balls he blocked, the third he glanced down the leg side past a fielder who was cleaning his spectacles.

"Run," called Luke.

"Go back," said the stranger.

"Crikey Sir, we want runs," complained Luke.

"Just make sure I keep the bowling and leave it to me," rejoined the stranger. "I'm just getting my eye in."

The next ball he lofted, with a fine wristy stroke, into a beech tree on the boundary.

"Six," exulted Luke.

The next shot was a solid drive through the covers, which found the boundary.

"Four."

The last ball of the over he placed just short of the boundary and walked a single. "I just can't run, got a 'knee'," he explained to Luke as they passed.

And so it went on. The stranger kept the bowling, and with a virtuoso display of stroke play won the match. He left the field perched high on Blackie's broad shoulder. Both teams lined up to applaud; the thirty or so spectators, all hardy followers of the game, raised a cheer; the sheep, sensing that their confinement was nearly over, joined in.

Luke insisted that Bob should receive the cup and keep it on his sideboard till next year.

Bob's second name was now on everyone's lips.

No . . . really . . . of Gloucester, and Somerset . . . and England. A County man . . . a test cricketer . . . on our pitch.

Bob's second name had of course been known to some, but only Mogford had guessed the cricket connection. The frequent private visits to the cricket field, the exceptional eye, the lightness of the step, and a Yorkshire terrier called Fred.

The brevity of the match day visits was perhaps, Mogford supposed, the offence to his purist soul of strokes badly played, poor technique, frustration at not being able to help. Well, he had spoken to Blackie about one or two things during the match.

When Mogford got to the pub the celebrations were in full swing. Blackie was about to make a speech.

He held up two large wicket keeping hands. "Quiet lads," he bellowed. He threw an affectionate arm round Bob's neck. "Us 'as, I think, been honoured today by a great cricketer." Cheers resounded. "Us needs a new President, and I think it would be a proper job if we asked Bob to honour us further by accepting the position."

The cheers were deafening and Bob's head in Blackie's armpit nodded weakly.

More cheers and Blackie said, "That's settled then. But," he went on, "Bob's down 'ere for peace and quiet to write 'is memoirs for a London publisher, so anyone who disturbs 'im, will answer to me personally." He glared all around. "Furthermore, any of you who think Bob is going to turn out for us is up a gum tree. Bob is seventy two and retired from the game. He is willing to coach youngsters, but not us old un's. Might spoil our fun."

Mogford intercepted a signal from Bob now looking like a prisoner in the pillory in Blackie's affectionate head lock.

"I'm taking Bob home now," he said. "Martha's getting a bit of supper for us."

They made for the door amid much back slapping and cheering.

"Don't be a stranger," called Blackie, "ee knows where to find us."

"Thanks for the rescue," whispered Bob. "I'm dead beat."

Near the door they encountered Luke, his face aglow from the effects of beer, hero worship, and the joys of victory.

Mogford put a hand on his shoulder. "You got it just right today lad. A nice blend of youth and experience."

* * *

Back at the farm Martha installed Bob in a comfortable chair in the kitchen.

"I thought you might like to rest first and have supper a little later on. I'll make a pot of tea to be going on with."

"I am a little tired," admitted Bob leaning back and closing his eyes.

When Martha appeared with the tea he was sleeping soundly. She drew Mogford aside. "There was a phone call from Miss Pringle. It seems Luke must have written to apologise for whatever it was that upset her."

"A bit of an effort for our Luke. He must quite like her," said Mogford. "What else did she say?"

"Well, she thanks him for his letter. Apology accepted. She says, she realised how much his cricket team means to him since he is prepared to fight for it."

"That's all m'dear?"

"Well only that she looks forward to seeing him in the summer and hopes that if he asks her out again it will not be so expensive for him."

"Best pass it on as it is and not ask too many questions," suggested Mogford. "Sleeping dogs and all that."

In the armchair Bob stirred and sat bolt upright. "Goodness," he said, "I didn't know where I was for a moment. Have we had supper?"

"Any minute now," said Mogford. "And you've certainly earned it."

* * *

Nobody talked of the 'stranger' now. It was Bob all the way. He became a regular visitor to the Mogford farm – perhaps encouraged by Martha's excellent suppers – and occasionally he would drop in at the pub. Here he was treated as one of the lads. He was grateful that he did not have to live up to celebrity status, and could just enjoy quiet conversation, a game of cards, a glass of beer.

There was, however, genuine interest in Bob's book due out before Christmas; especially as he had let it be known that he had included a chapter on village cricket in general as well as a piece on *their* annual local 'dust up'.

Martha was delighted that Bob had purchased Primrose Cottage and would now be a permanent part of the village community.

6
The pearly gates

AS the summer faded and falling leaves and a nip in the air brought a hint of autumn, Martha became a little concerned about Mogford. True the shortening days often seemed to put a damper on his spirits but not usually for long. Things would happen; the market was a place of infinite variety. Mogford was always getting involved. No time for moping.

He had mentioned Jimmy Wing once or twice recently, Martha remembered. He seemed to think Jimmy was not up to the mark. Yes she was sure that was it. He was worrying about Jimmy. Well it was market day. She could wait and see what transpired.

* * *

Mogford was not surprised to find Jimmy Wing in subdued mood. Jimmy, more often referred to as 'Wingie', was a drover in the market. A character noted for his repertoire of stock phrases, and normally ready to make a contribution to the quips and banter of market day. He was also extremely well informed, and Mogford, trading on many years of friendship, was often privy to useful information.

"There's a ring operating in the calf sales," Jimmy said. "Big dealers from up country; be here about two weeks."

"Thanks Jimmy; but what's amiss, you're not even smoking?"

Jimmy thought for a minute and seemed to come to a decision. "You know a few weeks ago there was an X-ray van outside the mart; well I was feeling a bit chesty so I went inside." He was silent for a time, then, "It seems I 'ave a shadow on me lungs."

Mogford could think of nothing to say, and a voice from the sale ring called . . . 'next'. Jimmy turned to let another bunch of store cattle into the passageway and Mogford watched as he drove them down to the ring.

"Come on m'dears, all together one at a time, right on there, one foot 'afore the other." The same old patter, but today it had a hollow ring.

Mogford had some thinking to do. There was the question of the dealers. Next week he had calves to buy for a client. He had already agreed a price and had planned to buy from a lady breeder, whose calves, due in the market next week, would be in prime condition. He tried to apply his mind to it, but Jimmy Wing kept filling his thoughts.

He could remember him going off to war; a tall slim lad, the wartime marriage which lasted such a short time and had left him with a daughter (his little flower). He came back with a D.C.M. but short of most of his left arm and some of his senses. He did not talk about his decoration, and few people were aware of his service record. He was Wingie, the drover. He lived in a mean street near the market. He was by most people's standards a little strange. He roamed the countryside, took a fish here, a rabbit there, netted elvers in the season, and could find congers in rock holes. His predations were never excessive, and were tolerated. His mother, now dead, had brought Jimmy's daughter up in the faith, and she, after training as a nurse, had gone off to serve in a medical mission in China. His job in the market was now perhaps the most stable thing in Jimmy's life.

Through the café window Mogford could see him at

work. Tall and looking thin and stooped in middle age, a short knobbly stick tucked under his stump as he opened a gate one handed, his oilskins spattered in muck. Mogford got to his feet. There were things to be done. He must waylay Jimmy's postman and make a few calls in the town.

Mogford made his way to the calf sales. The strangers were not hard to spot. Three in number, crchestrated by a very large imposing figure. Perhaps forty five years of age, he stood well over six feet and bulked out in every direction. A large beaming heavily chinned face was topped off with a check shooting hat on a very small head. A stout walking stick hung from the breast pocket of his tweed jacket and his bright blue gimlet eyes missed nothing.

Standing near the auctioneer he shared his view of the bidders, and it was clear to Mogford that these three would pay a bit over the odds to get the bulk of the calves. Sometimes a local would push too hard and end up paying more than he intended. Occasionally the large dealer would reprimand the auctioneer for plucking bids out of the air. "And where did you get that yin auctioneer," he would beam.

"Over there . . . was that a bid Sir, no, sorry, well back to you Sir . . ." Soon the locals would drift away, and the 'ring' would have it all their own way.

Big buyers from the Midlands, reasoned Mogford, and he was intrigued that the big man had an accent like Martha's. Mogford decided to abandon the market, make a few calls, and have a long talk with Martha.

* * *

To Martha the market was an alien place, far removed from the classrooms of her earlier years. It was a place too full of rough masculinity, noise, bustle, spattering muck, profanity, and, she suspected, sharp practice. But here she was, a week later, walking towards the calf ring. Why, she wondered, did she let Mogford talk her into these things.

Mogford himself was practically in disguise; bare headed, a long loose mackintosh and polished black shoes. "Now you know what you have to do," he hissed as they neared the ring.

"Yes, I think so," quavered Martha.

The dealers were already on station, but the ringside was only thinly populated. Mogford with apparent roughness thrust Martha against the rails beside the large dealer. "And don't forget," he said fiercely, "I want ten red heifer calves from her Ladyship's load, and you know what I'll pay for them. Get it right or you'll hear about it." With that he stalked off.

"Wrong side o' the bed," suggested the big man smiling down at her.

"Aye, you could say that," said Martha. In her terror her careful Morningside accent was slipping.

"You're from Scotland," he chuckled, "well I never, which part? Edinburgh? Really? Do you know . . .?"

Martha was beginning to feel more at ease.

A youth struggling with a recalcitrant calf in the background was cursing freely.

The dealer fixed him with a stern eye. "Here laddie mind the language, lady present."

"Sorry missus," said the youth touching his cap, "it's just that this bloody calf . . ."

The moment of truth was at hand and Martha's panic was rapidly reasserting itself. There was a red calf in the ring and the bidding had started. At the appointed price Martha's hand shot up. "Steady missus, that's a bull calf," the big man spoke up. "Not a bid auctioneer, the lady was waving to someone." He leaned down. "What you need is a signal, get in early on the next one, catch the auctioneer's eye and give the strap of your shoulder bag a tweak. My lot will keep out, the locals think they are bidding against me. Just don't go over your price, and," he grinned, "make sure it's a heifer."

Martha got to work; soon she was beginning to enjoy herself.

* * *

Later, when they met at the prearranged rendezvous in town, Mogford noticed the lightness of Martha's mood.

"You've had a good day?" he suggested.

"Splendid," said Martha.

"You got the calves?"

"Just as you ordered," replied Martha.

"And the dealers, did they help?" Mogford was intrigued.

"Oh yes, the large gentleman comes from Edinburgh, apparently his sister and I went to the same school. He took me up the town for tea and we talked and talked. It was lovely. And by the way Mogford, I don't think he was fooled for a moment by all that cloak and dagger stuff this morning. I think he just liked me."

"Well m'dear," Mogford smiled, "that was my ace card; I knew I couldn't fail on that one. Let's go home."

On the way home Martha said, "There's just one thing Mogford."

"Yes m'dear?"

"When I was needing my last calf a pair came in the ring. It seems they were twins and her Ladyship wouldn't part them."

"So," said Mogford.

"So I agreed with her."

Mogford only too well aware of Martha's Achilles heel, grinned. "One for us then m'dear."

* * *

It was three weeks later. The up country dealers had gone. Things were back to normal. Even 'Wingie' seemed more his usual self. He was servicing the fat cattle sale. The butchers were round the ring.

"How are you Jimmy?" asked Mogford.

"Happier," said 'Wingie'. "My liddle old flower's coming home."

"That's great news Jimmy, she'll take care of you," Mogford beamed.

"Oh ah," Jimmy gave Mogford a knowing look. "It seems that women's groups hereabouts want her to lecture and they will help her raise funds for the mission. The hospice have offered her work. It seems she's needed here, and just in case ee had 'ort to do wi' it, here's a present." He produced from an inside pocket a fish that would not have disgraced a banquet at the Imperial.

Mogford realised that such a fine specimen could represent two weeks wages to Jimmy Wing.

"They can spare it where it came from," 'Wingie' said simply and producing a sheet of greaseproof from another pocket he handed the wrapped fish to Mogford.

"Thanks Jimmy." Mogford knew when to accept a gift. "And how's the chest?" he enquired.

"Not good, it's no use pretending."

"Well," said Mogford, "they can do a lot these days."

"Not for me, not now, I can feel that liddle old tap on the arse, down the passage . . . next." He turned away to open a gate. A young steer plodded obediently past. "No more chance than that liddle ole dear. Anyway that's the way it is Mr Mogford both for beast an' man." He strode off after the steer, tapping lightly. "All together one at a time, don't shit 'afore ee gets on the scales, right on ole flower . . ." There was something symbolic in the clang of the gate and the voices more faintly in the ring.

"What have we here Jimmy?"

"The best liddle ole steer in the market."

Mogford walked away, the echo of the slammed gate still in his consciousness; the note of finality depressed him; the door of a dungeon slamming on a prisoner; the knell of doom . . . but . . . no he musn't think like that. It was the pearly gates with St Peter on the other side enquiring, 'what have we here then?' Mogford looked around the market. This was his place; the sale rings, the pens, animals, people, lorries; some youths knobbling in a corner; the café would be agog with gossip; the pub across the road would soon be full of laughter. Some of these fine animals would walk up to their pearly gates today, the stores would walk through to green pasture. They would be bought to feed on a bit longer. They would live. The butcher's beast would not. The same for beast and man Jimmy had said.

Mogford turned to look at him doing his job; a poacher of other people's fish, a man with his own morality. He watched as Jimmy tucked the little stick under his stump, undid the gate one handed, a little tap to let his charge know he was there and then the voice, cajoling, comforting – 'all together one at a time, right on . . .'

And then another sound broke upon Mogford's ears. Listening to Jimmy, it was as if the rest of the market had stood silently in the background awaiting his attention. Now he became aware of its voice. A muted sound, swelling and fading like a distant orchestra; a heartbeat, slow but vibrant, full of life. Mogford looked and listened for a time. He could feel the energy of the place. There was life here; a vitality that was infectious. And the noise. It was music in his ears. He grabbed the arm of a youth standing near him. "Can you hear it?" he said excitedly. "It's like a great orchestra."

The youth turned puzzled eyes on him.

"What do you hear?" demanded Mogford.

"Nort," said the lad. "Only cattle shittin' and men swearin'."

"That's all, it doesn't sound like music to you?"

"Are you all right Mr Mogford?" enquired the youth anxiously.

"Fine, fine," said Mogford.

The young man walked away, shaking his head.

Mogford looked across at 'Wingie'. He seemed to be listening too. Mogford signalled good luck with a brief thumbs up. Jimmy Wing made a silent gesture towards his cap with his knobby stick; then both men turned about their business.

* * *

Martha was quick to sense Mogford's mood. "You do look downhearted," she said. "Let's get those market boots off you, and I'll get you a nice cup of tea. Supper won't be long." She looked at him anxiously. "What is it? Is it Jimmy Wing?"

"No, at least not entirely." He started to undo his boots. "Jimmy's not too good of course, in fact he might be quite ill, but no . . . there's something else."

"Not those silly rumours about a new road through the village is it? Motorways, dual carriageways, road widening. All that's a long way off, if ever. There's no more to it than that talk of London overspill coming down here." She handed Mogford a cup of tea. "Is that it my dear?" she asked.

"I wish it was," said Mogford. "I really do. No, it's closer to home than that, and I hardly know how to tell you."

Martha came to sit on the arm of his chair. "You'd better start at the beginning," she said gently. "Just tell me all about it. We've had problems before and survived."

"Well," said Mogford slowly. "I was just leaving the market when I bumped into Jim Passmore . . ."

"The dealer," Martha interrupted. "I thought you didn't care much for him. Isn't he a bit . . . well . . . on the shifty side?"

"He has a bit of a reputation for sailing close to the wind, and it is true I don't like him much, and I wouldn't have any dealings with him but there he was, and I had to stop and have a word."

"And?"

"Well, it seems he is buying up Red Devon cattle for shipment to Argentina . . ."

"Surely not your kind of business Mogford, is it? Where's the problem?"

"No that doesn't worry me," replied Mogford. "But he is recruiting a stockman to go with them, and this lad has the promise of a good job where the cattle are going . . . and that's my worry."

"Go on Mogford, I can feel the bad news coming, just put it into words."

Mogford sighed and nodded. "I think you know what I am going to say, he's approached Luke."

Martha moved over to a chair and sank heavily into it. "Get me a cup of tea Mogford, or better still a drop of that medicinal whisky I keep in the cupboard. I just hope Luke isn't tempted, that's all; has he said anything?"

"That's just it," replied Mogford grimly. "I understand from Passmore that he is considering it."

"But Luke has said nothing, not even a hint."

"I expect he doesn't want to worry us, until it's all cut and dried. After all if it doesn't come off . . . well anyway we wouldn't be worrying now if I hadn't bumped into Passmore. I think he enjoyed telling me. I don't trust the man, he might do the dirty on Luke once the cattle are delivered and paid for. He's just the sort to go back on his word."

"Well it's out in the open now, we'll have to talk it over with Luke at supper. I don't look forward to that; I think I know what his answer to Passmore will be. He's been a bit restless lately. When will he go?"

"As soon as the cattle are bought, I understand," replied Mogford glumly. "It could be before Christmas."

"Oh surely not, Mogford. That poor lad in a foreign place for Christmas. I can't bear the thought."

"It won't be the same here without him, at Christmas . . . or any other time come to that," said Mogford. "I think I hear him crossing the yard. We'll soon know. Anyway m'dear, whatever, you can depend on me to do the best I can to keep him here."

"I have a lot of faith in you Mogford, I shall expect you to keep him here for me."

7
The Red Devons

IT was just two weeks before Christmas and Mogford and Martha had been living with their bad news for four days; their worst fears had been confirmed over supper that fateful evening.

Mogford was at his wits end. He had hoped the cattle buying might have hit a few snags, but it was going like a dream. Plenty of cattle forward and prices favouring the buyer. He began to think there was nothing left but prayer, and anyway Martha was hard at it in that direction. If things went on the way they were going, the cattle would be on the water in a matter of days, and Luke with them.

Mogford was in the yard when Martha's prayers were answered. Something landed on his nose, cold and soft, and then another and another. It was snowing.

The next morning all roads were blocked. Not a cattle lorry in the area could turn a wheel. Passmore phoned to say the shipment had been postponed until the weather cleared. Meantime he had his lairage full of hungry cattle which had to be fed and he had missed a sailing. Worse still, the prospect for collecting cattle still lodged on remote farms, was dependent on a rapid change in the weather. Even if the weather were to clear it would take time to arrange for another ship. And the weather didn't clear, if anything it got worse. Mogford and Martha bore the inconvenience with rare fortitude. They had been given a little more time. Martha was quite sure who had granted it.

Truth to tell Mogford had been caught out a little by this early fall. With his mind on other things he had let his stock of pig food get low and this was now critical. He had five days to think of something. Perhaps the main roads would be clear soon. Mogford was reluctant to ask Martha to use her good offices to ask for one road to be cleared just to suit him, when she was assiduously praying that all roads should be blocked to cattle transport for as long as possible.

Meantime Luke had a problem of buried sheep. He explained his strategy over supper after a day of effort and preparation.

"It's God's will," said Martha philosophically as she ladled hot soup.

"Well I wish he had given some thought to the extra work he has caused us, not to mention the poor sheep that might die if I don't find them," grumbled Luke.

"And there's the pig food," said Mogford.

"It's lack of planning," said Martha unsympathetically. "You Luke could have had the sheep in shelter, and you, Mogford, I keep telling you not to let the feed stock run too low. Anyhow there'll be nothing moving on the roads for a day or two yet."

"Meantime," said Mogford, turning to Luke. "Now we have been put in our places what have you done about the sheep?"

"The sheep have done a lot for themselves really," said Luke. "They had drifted up to that wood at the top of the farm for shelter, but of course some are buried. I'll find them with Rip in the morning. I found a way up with the tractor and have made straw bale shelters, and they have some fodder. By the way I saw some smoke going up further into the wood, like somebody had lit a fire. I didn't have time to go over. I'll take a look in the morning."

"You've done well Luke," said Mogford. "I still have my pig feed to sort out. I need something to change."

And change something did. The next morning Luke came in for breakfast to report a change in the weather.

"Surely not a thaw," said Martha anxiously.

Luke reassured her on that point. "Quite the opposite," he said. "In fact there's a bit of frost, and in the night the wind has blown a lot of snow off the fields."

"Into the lanes hopefully," suggested Martha.

"That's dead right," said Luke. "In fact the roads will be worse, except perhaps that top road. It sits above a slope and might have blown itself a bit clearer." Luke moved over to the window. "The deep snow has blown off the field opposite, with this touch of frost it would be just right for sledging."

"You just keep your mind on your work, young Luke," said Martha severely. "There's all those poor sheep, and maybe somebody sheltering in the wood up there. Just remember there is no such thing as trespassing in this weather. Whoever is up there will need a good meal. There'll be something here, whoever it is."

"You're the boss. I know the house rules." Luke grinned cheerfully. "Fancy a bit of sledging tonight Da'?"

Mogford had been very thoughtful throughout breakfast. He brightened. "I might at that," he smiled. "Yes, I might enjoy that."

Luke trudged up the slope to the wood, Rip zig zagging to heel. If he saw smoke this morning he intended to investigate. He looked back. Below him nestling in the valley was the farmhouse; smoke curling upwards in the sharp morning air gave a promise of warmth inside. He would miss it; Ma and Da', his friends and Miss Pringle – Betty – would be down in the summer. He felt he owed her something. He should try to make up to her for his bad behaviour; she had been in his thoughts quite a bit of late, but there, a man had to make a move sometime. He might only stay six months, see what it was like, earn some money. It would be nice to feel more independent, not always walking in his father's shadow. He might marry one day. Yes he would marry one day – but not yet awhile.

Bringing himself back from his reverie he looked at the field opposite. It was always a good sled run. Steep, but flattening out at the bottom. It was a good long run as well. If he wasn't too tired he might just give it a go tonight.

As he looked, a rotund figure appeared on the slope, making heavy weather of his journeying.

I wonder what Da's up to, maybe heading for the top road to see if a lorry might get through. Even if he got his pig food to the top of that field, I doubt if the tractor would make it up the slope. Still pondering, Luke reached the wood. Smoke was rising. He plodded in that direction.

Without knowing what to expect, Luke was still surprised at the sight which met his eyes. It was an encampment of some elaboration. Swiftly Luke absorbed the scene. The hut was of branches over which a tarpaulin had been stretched. A thick layer of leaves, and a foot or so of snow gave the appearance of an igloo. Luke's engineering eye assessed the 'U' value as being high. He guessed the hut had been erected before the snow, covered with dead leaves to give a measure of insulation, and in the night mother nature had donated the snow.

The man squatting by the fire in the doorway seemed happy enough with his lot. He smiled broadly, strong white teeth, in a slightly swarthy face. Dark eyes which twinkled.

"Hello maister," he called in greeting as Luke approached.

"Hello yourself," Luke grinned. "All alone?"

The man looked around. "Can't see anybody else unless ee count the donkey." He indicated a rough shelter. "Ee's behind that windbreak. I wasn't sure if ee would behave in the hut." He grinned broadly. "I'm not trespassin' am I?"

"I suppose you are in a way," said Luke. "But my mother says you have to come to supper so I expect that makes it all right. I'll see you later then, I'll come for you before I go home. Who are you anyway?"

"Well, that's real nice o' ee'r mother. I'm Ben Loverage. Gipsy Ben Loverage in full. I got caught out by this 'ere storm; like a lot of folk I dare say. What are ee doin', I don't suppose ee came up here just to ask me for supper?"

"Buried sheep," said Luke briefly. "There's a lot of work to do. Rip here is good at finding them, that helps."

"Then I'll work for my supper. Me and Barty."

"Barty?"

"The donkey," explained Ben. He's as old as I am. I called him Bartholomew, but it was too much of a mouthful, he seems happy enough with Barty. He's used to carrying, us could use 'im as a pack animal."

The work went on apace. Barty with an improvised rope harness could carry two sheep to the one each of the humans. By nightfall Luke reckoned that all the sheep had been accounted for. He was well pleased with the team effort, and felt that both Ben and Barty had earned their supper.

The small cavalcade moved out of the wood. Barty the donkey was going to share a bale of hay with Daisy. Ben, Luke felt, had earned a huge supper, and perhaps a few drinks, at the very least. As for himself . . . well, he was well pleased with the day's work, and not too tired for a frolic on the slope of the field opposite. There was enough light for him to see that there was just the right amount of snow, and this little nip of frost . . . it would be perfect.

And what was that? At the top of the field . . . a lorry? A loaded lorry? The pig food?

Soon the streaming light from the farmhouse windows offered welcome, with a hint of comfort and good food within, but first Ben had to see to his donkey.

The cowshed had an animal warmth about it. Barty hee-hawed his approval and Daisy viewed him with lowered lids, before turning back to the job of packing her rumen with sweet smelling hay.

"Looks like they might get on," suggested Luke. "Tether the little chap up beside Daisy. They can share a stall, and there's enough hay for two."

Luke's day of surprises was not yet over. Supper was on the go all right, and Martha greeted Ben like a long lost brother, but the mince pies! Every available surface was covered with mince pies, and there were more in the Aga.

"A bit early for Christmas, isn't it Ma?"

"Just you wait and see, young Luke. Come on sit yourselves down, have a cup of tea to be going on with, your father won't be long."

"But where is he? Not like him to be late for supper. And what's he up to?"

"You can ask him yourself in a minute, I can hear his step."

A rapid patter of feet heralded the arrival of Mogford in the kitchen. His beaming face signalled goodwill to all men. He rubbed his hands. "A fine night for a bit of sledging," he enthused. "Just perfect. Couldn't be better."

"I have to agree with all that," said Luke, with just a hint of exasperation. "But what's going on? Oh, and this is Ben Loverage. He's been digging for sheep all day."

Mogford shook hands. "Then you must stay with us till this snow clears, you are welcome, and of course it goes without saying you will enjoy the party with us tonight."

"Party!" Luke was more than a little impatient now. "Will someone please tell me what's going on, what kind of party, with all the roads blocked."

"Go on Mogford. Put the boy out of his misery. Tell him about the tobogganing party you've arranged."

"I still call it sledging," said Mogford.

"Tobogganing is the word nowadays," said Martha primly.

"Oh for goodness sake, what does it matter, what's this all in aid of?"

"Put like that," said Mogford. "It's in aid of getting my pigfood from the top of the hill to the bottom, where it can be loaded on to a trailer."

"I noticed the load," said Luke slowly, the strategy beginning to shape up in his mind. "Who's coming, the whole village I should think by the number of mince pies. And I suppose everybody will put a bag on the sledge, sit on top and whizz down; seems like a bit of fun, what do you say Ben?"

"I'm game for anything," grinned Ben. "Many hands do make light work they do say. But what about 'Mother' 'ere? There's the washing up and getting ready for this ole party; I think I'd better stop 'ere and 'elp."

Luke grinned. "I'm sure Ma isn't going to say no to that offer, are you Ma?"

"I certainly am not. It's seldom enough I get any help around here. Now hurry yourselves up, Ben and I have lots to do."

Supper was hardly over before lights appeared at the top of the field. Someone had produced torches which flamed bravely on the end of poles.

"Looks like a meeting of the Ku-Klux-Klan," said Luke. "I'd better get up there and set the ball rolling. I expect you'll see to the tractor at the bottom?" He cocked a quizzical eye at his father.

"Somebody's got to see to the dull routine," grinned Mogford. "At least the pigs will have some food tomorrow. Somebody up there must be looking after us." He rolled his eyes heavenwards.

Martha looked at him sternly. "He's helped you out this time Mogford, don't forget we have another problem. He might need a little help from you on that one. Now off you go, get out from under my feet, all of you, except Ben of course."

Presently, resting from their labours, Ben and Martha stood by the window.

"It's quite a sight," said Martha. "Mogford never does things by halves."

Ben had to agree. The sky seemed to be doing its bit, with stars ablaze and a three quarter moon shedding light and casting shadows. Torch poles had been fixed to sledges and naked flames streamed backwards. Children held sparklers, some, riding the sledges adding to the fairytale quality of it all. Shouts and screams and laughter, and at the bottom of the hill Mogford with a rapidly increasing number of bags on his trailer. He was a happy man, his friends were having the time of their lives. He was getting his pig food; there was just one shadow over it all; he would have to do something about Luke. He had some thinking to do.

"They'll soon be coming in at this rate, those sledges are going ever so fast, don't you think Ben?"

"Luke said it was proper for sledging," said Ben. "Can I get some beer ready?"

His question was answered by the sound of boots being kicked free of snow and Blackie's head round the door. He was carrying a keg of his special.

"They'll be all in in a minute, I thought I might be the first to a beer, or maybe the cider," he grinned happily. "What a night, the sledging was great."

"It's not over yet," said Martha. "There's all those mince pies to eat up."

"They'll soon go," said Blackie as a rush of feet, and excited voices, announced the arrival of the main body of helpers.

Blackie had organised his cricketers; Bob arrived later to enjoy a mince pie and the company; Percy was enthusiastic. "Nearly as much fun as riding point-to-point," but he couldn't stay too long, Belinda was alone with the baby.

And so the festivities progressed. Ben had a few conjuring tricks, Mogford brought the company up to date with the latest jokes. Blackie made a speech and the mince pies disappeared in time with the drinks. The evening was voted a success by all. Not least by Mogford. But this other thing . . . he must think of something.

* * *

The next morning saw little change in the weather.

Ben had been a little drunk the night before. He wasn't used to such convivial company and he and Blackie had hit it off rather well. He was rubbing his eyes when he came down to breakfast. "What were that stuff we was drinking last night?" he enquired of Martha. Indeed Martha was the only one around apart from Hammy; the others had gone about their chores.

"Scrumpy," said Martha, smiling indulgently on him. "You must have come across it in Somerset. Although," she added thoughtfully, "perhaps not the same as surviving Blackie's home brew; it has a reputation . . . well, try some breakfast, and don't drink any water, they say it starts it all up again."

"Well 'Mother', I just isn't used to it, more of a beer man myself."

And as he explained while picking disinterestedly at his food, he was not used to regular routine hours. "It's like this, 'Mother'," he said. "If I is to live this reg'lar life, for a day or two like, then I 'ave to do some reg'lar work. And I 'avn't seen to my donkey yet. I always feeds him 'fore I eats."

"Don't worry about your donkey, Ben, I saw him when I milked Daisy. He's been quite happy sharing a stall and they have plenty of fodder to go at. He seems to be enjoying the change."

"Come to that, so am I," said Ben. "But I know my feet'll itch sooner or later and I will 'ave to be off. Maybe I could muck out the cowshed?"

"Too late I think, all done," smiled Martha.

Ben thought for a moment and then slapped a hand on

his thigh. "I got it! I got it! My trade, I sharpen knives; do you bring all they blunt knives, scissors, axes, hedging tools, I'll put an edge on 'em. I never knowed a farmer yet but he had blunt tools. I'll get the ole donkey cart down 'ere wi' me tackle. Eh, where shall I work?"

"In here, where it's warm," suggested Martha, not at all sure that she wanted Ben to get his hands on her best cutlery. "I'll get the farm tools, and maybe the carving knives."

Martha watched Ben and Barty set off to get the cart. Ben wasn't all that steady, she thought, Blackie's cider was an acquired ability. Come to think of it Blackie seemed to be the only one who could handle more than a small glass.

Ben's equipment was home made and soon set in place. Martha watched in some trepidation as he wheeled in a bike and set a back wheel stand in its place. This kept the back wheel clear of the floor. A grindstone mounted on the handlebars was driven by a belt which operated on a pulley fixed to the back wheel. Ben, pedalling, would provide the power.

"Coffee first," insisted Martha. "I don't see you on that wobbly bike just yet, coffee and a chat first. Sit you down."

Martha studied the swarthy face bent over the mug of coffee, drinking gratefully, both hands around its warmth. Dark eyes that twinkled a lot and matched the mane of black hair; the good teeth that showed so prominently when he smiled. A real Romany, she decided.

"I 'ave real Romany blood," said Ben quietly.

Martha started. "Are you a mind reader as well? I was just having thoughts along those lines."

"Most folk do," he smiled. "Loverage be a well known name in Somerset, a famous gipsy name, real Romany. I 'ave pure Romany blood, both sides."

Martha was impressed. "Have you never lived in a house?" she wanted to know.

"I do live in a house sometimes," said Ben. "Back in Somerset. Barty has a shed on the allotment."

"But the hut in the woods, I thought . . ." Martha was nonplussed.

"Just me and Barty on our holidays. It's a long story, are you sure you wants to 'ear it?"

Martha did, and listening got a new insight into this strange man, so driven by his Romany blood yet prepared to compromise for the love of a woman.

It seemed that, twenty years ago when he was twenty two he fell in love with a delicate young non gipsy called Maria. They married against the wishes of both sets of parents, and indeed Maria being only nineteen, married without the consent of her parents. They were blissfully happy for a short time despite the family problems, but soon Ben's itchy feet took him travelling. Only short trips and not too often, but Maria was miserable without him and elected to go on a trip and share the hardships.

Ben paused at this point. There was a sadness in his eyes and his thoughts were elsewhere. Drifting backwards down the years.

"And something happened," suggested Martha gently.

Ben nodded. "It were a spell of weather such as this. I got caught out like, well . . . same as this time really, nob'dy was prepared for this 'ere lot. But Barty and me we're tough as old boots. She was delicate see, not used to it. She caught pneumonia and just went down and down, and she left us for good. Just a poor wisp of a thing at the end; all big eyes and yellow hair. I should never 'ave took 'er from 'er parents, it were wrong, she were never right for a gipsy life and I were no good to 'er; but we 'ave 'ot blood us gipsies, I followed me 'eart, and so did she. But it was never right, I knows that now. I should 'ave married a strong gipsy girl and 'ad strong children. She poor thing could 'ave married a bank manager and been safe and cared for. I blames myself. For twenty years I've blamed myself."

"And your family, couldn't you go back? Live with the tribe again, travel. Surely you don't have to be alone?"

"That's what I gived up for love," said Ben sadly. "They cast me out. I be a non-gipsy now. It's just me and Barty now. I do pick up a bit of work here and there, enough to live on and a bit of fodder for Barty, and us do go travelling when the mood takes us." He smiled. "A sad tale 'Mother'. Now I must earn my keep."

Saddened by Ben's misfortune Martha went about her chores and left Ben to his work. The sound of stone on steel was testimony to his industry. It was the erratic whistling and occasional bursts of ribald song that finally drew her to the kitchen.

Ben was in full song, and in top gear. The spokes blurred and the sparks flew, and a half empty jug was at his elbow.

"Ben," called Martha, horror in her voice. "That knife, it's Mogford's favourite carving knife."

Ben slowed and examined the knife. "Just a bit uneven in one place. I'll soon take that off." He resumed his activities with gusto.

"Ben," wailed Martha. "I warned you about the water." She snatched the jug away. "I think you've done enough, maybe more than enough. Just let's call it a day."

Martha's displeasure had a sobering effect on Ben. "Not maybe the best job I 'as ever done. But they be proper sharp." He felt an edge gingerly. "I do think Maistr'll be pleased."

Martha doubted that. She was looking out of the window. "I see you have your tarpaulin on the cart," she said.

Ben got down from his precarious perch and joined her. "It be like this 'Mother'," he said. "Me and Barty, we have to be a journeying on. I reck'n us can get up through that field opposite, an' the road up there a'nt too bad. When I went up to the ole camp in the woods to fetch me cart, I knowed us must be movin' on. It's our life see,

'Mother' . . . travellin', it's in the blood I reck'n."

"Well at least you will take enough food for the day and a bale of hay for Barty." Martha said firmly.

"Put like that 'Mother' how can I refuse, a passel o' bread and cheese be a proper job for me, and Barty do thank ee as well. He'll miss your Daisy and that warm cowshed I reck'n."

"But you'll pass this way again," said Martha. "Come when the wood is full of bluebells, you're welcome down here or in the wood, however the spirit moves you."

"I'll get me cart ready," said Ben.

Martha watched them cross the field zig zagging against the steep slope; Barty digging in manfully with his dainty feet, Ben hauling on a rope, doing his share. And then they were at the top and passing through the gate and out of sight. There was no sound drifting back, snow masked the clip-clop of hooves, the rattle of wheels, there was only a ghostly silence. It was as if they had passed through the gate and disappeared off the face of the earth.

And then a hee-haw broke the silence, a loud exuberant sound and then the sound of Ben whistling.

Martha smiled, there was a kind of happiness in the sounds, man and beast, they were the travelling kind, and they were travelling.

It was later that evening with Mogford about to carve the joint, that he noticed something. "This is not my usual knife," he complained.

"Oh yes it is," replied Martha. "It's been sharpened."

"Ben?" Mogford wanted to know. "Anything else?"

"Only a few more knives . . . and your hedging tools."

"The same?"

Martha nodded. "All smaller and lighter, but sharp. Ben guarantees the sharpness."

"Perhaps he never visits the same place twice," mused Mogford.

"I think we should give him the benefit of the doubt,"

said Martha with a smile. "Let's put it down to the cider."

* * *

Martha was at a loss to understand it. Mogford was planning another big party for the Saturday before Christmas. She had a feeling that he was up to something. Mogford was a 'party' man, she knew that, but, well, they had just had the sledging party, and then there was the expense. Mogford was always most careful not to spend beyond their means. Yes, there was something at the back of all this, he had been making phone calls . . . Martha decided she must go along with it and wait and see.

As per usual breakfast time turned into a planning meeting, as it invariably did when a project was afoot.

"We'll have a buffet in the house and the dance in the barn," decided Mogford. "We shall need a stage Luke, and some heating, curtains for the stage, some decorations, holly, a few streamers . . ."

"The stage . . . easy, poultry crates with some chipboard cladding, straw bales round the edges for a rustic look." Luke was curious. "Are we having a band then?"

"Sounds like a posh do," observed Martha. "I expect there will be a lot of cooking to do?"

"Just your usual m'dear, I'll get some of the ladies from the village to help. Now about heating, Luke."

"I expect I could borrow some space heaters, you know, the sort they have in potato stores. No I don't think that will be a problem. Leave the barn to me Da', I'll fix it up. You just do the interesting bits. This band though, must be setting you back a bit."

"Well," said Mogford, thinking quickly. "I didn't go to Smithfield this year, that saved a bit . . ."

"Say no more," Luke interrupted. "That would easily cover it, what do you say Ma?"

"I would say it is better spending money down here on

our friends than wasting it in those iniquitous places up in London."

Mogford felt the conversation had taken a dangerous turn and having suddenly discovered he had 'hundreds to do' he beat a hasty retreat.

There seemed little doubt that a thaw was on the way and by the Saturday the snow had virtually all gone. Mogford was glad of this and in fact had been in close contact with the local RAF weather station who had forecast this as a strong possibility. Great care had gone into the selection of the band. Many telephone calls had been made, friends consulted, agencies approached, and the final selection would be travelling up from South Devon. Road conditions had been Mogford's big worry.

He went to inspect the barn. Luke had been in his element. Nobody could have guessed that the stage was supported by a layer of poultry crates. It crossed Mogford's mind that Luke might not have taken the time to pressure wash them first but he wasn't going to ask at this stage. Paper decorations and holly bedecked the walls – Mogford could see Martha's hand in this and space heaters pointed like cannons through strategic apertures. At the far end of the barn stood a handcart with a huge cask of cider on board. Blackie could almost guarantee a convivial evening by greeting arrivals with a small glass of his special brew. Mogford was well pleased. He knew Martha and her helpers would be on top of arrangements indoors. He also knew that Martha didn't like flying blind. She hadn't argued about the expense, she was going along with him, trusting him. It was a very long shot but it was all he had. He hoped it would come off. If it didn't he had some explaining to do.

* * *

The food had been excellent; people were drifting into the barn to be accosted by Blackie, his face already aglow with goodwill. The cider barrel was tapped and guests were being offered small glasses of Blackie's best. Many negative gestures could be observed but Blackie's hospitality was hard to resist. The conversation noise levels grew and the band could be heard tuning up behind the curtains.

Luke in his role of chief stage manager was standing by, the control cords in his capable hands.

The band had gone through the squeaks and groans of tuning up and shuffling feet indicated a move to stations. A voice was heard, one, two, three, four and the music burst forth. Luke pulled the cords and the curtains parted to reveal the musicians in all the glory of smart livery.

They played briskly and people danced with a degree of enthusiasm depending on whether they had had one glass or two of the welcoming cider.

The dance was soon over, just a warm up for the band and a few early revellers. Luke still stood by the stage, fascinated by the glitter and colour of it all. An observant person might have seen an almost imperceptible sale ring type signal pass between Mogford and the band leader. The musicians sorted through their music sheets and started to play, soft and slow.

From behind the side curtains appeared a vision sheathed in shimmering silver, with long smooth blonde hair and eyes that were soft and liquid enough for any susceptible young man to drown in. She was by far the most beautiful woman Luke had ever seen, even on the films.

The vision stepped up to the microphone and started to sing. Her voice was low and seductive. "Come to me my melancholy baby," she sang, her voice hardly above a whisper, intimate and personal, and her eyes devouring Luke. "Cuddle up and don't be blue." Her arms were cuddling the air around her but her eyes never left Luke's face. Luke was already drowning in those liquid eyes. He found himself walking towards the stage as if in a dream. This was pure Hollywood. He was on the stage and the vision was holding his hands and singing to him and for him. He was aware of a heady perfume, the nearness of her perfect body and . . . someone was tugging at his sleeve.

It was Mogford. "I've just taken a phone call for you. It's Passmore. The trip's on. He wants an answer. What shall I tell him?"

Luke turned glazed eyes on his father. "How about no," he said.

* * *

"Wasn't it lucky that Passmore phoned just when he did," beamed Martha, in a seventh heaven about Luke's decision.

Luke's heroic evening had left them rather exhausted and they were having a lie in.

"Well, wasn't it?" she demanded.

Mogford was looking a little uneasy. "Well it didn't actually come just then. I delivered it just then," he explained.

"Well when did it come?" Martha was beginning to see the light.

"The day before, actually, on the Friday. I just chose my time, there didn't seem any point in rushing things."

"And that girl, Mogford – where did you produce her from?"

"Contacts," said Mogford. "Actually I know her father, had a deal or two with him. The girl's an actress, well something of a singer as well. In fact she has just landed a part as understudy in a big new musical on the London stage. She'll be off to London almost right away."

"So, an actress, and a pretty good one I would say, got the looks as well, got everything in fact. I wasn't too happy about all that cheek to cheek dancing with our Luke though."

"Last night was probably one of her best performances," Mogford said.

"Perhaps it was all acting," suggested Martha. "But if it *was* a performance I expect you had to pay."

"Let's just say I might have to miss Smithfield next year as well."

"You old fox," said Martha, but there was warmth in her voice and gratitude, and admiration and love. "You're a dear," she added and held out her arms.

8

A bit of business

THINGS had a way of sorting themselves out, thought Mogford, as he pulled up in the market car park. He was looking forward to his day. Old friends to chat to, maybe a little deal here and there; getting back in the swim with the Christmas troubles some weeks behind him.

It had come to his ears that Passmore's replacement for Luke had fared badly. The promised fine job hadn't materialised, an empty promise, a carrot to attract a stockman. The young man in question had apparently found work of a sort in a stockyard and was saving what he could against his fare home.

Luke had settled down quite happily, his night of glitz and glamour a cherished memory, but a note had come for him in the post, promising tickets for the show and a visit backstage. Perhaps it had not been all one sided.

But Mogford realised that Miss Pringle was not out of the running. There was that telephone call he had overheard. Luke trying to justify his change of plan. 'Dodgy operator – could have been a disaster. Yes he agreed with her, he ought to be a bit more independent. Of course he was looking forward to seeing her in the summer. No, he hadn't broken any pub furniture recently. He had turned over a new leaf.'

Mogford thought that perhaps he owed it to Luke to expand the business, get into a bigger league, make life a bit more exciting for him; perhaps even a bit of export; yes he would think that one over.

As he walked into the market he met Bob Pettit one of the two auctioneers who operated in the mart.

They exchanged greetings. "Much in today?" asked Mogford.

"About usual," said Pettit. "A bit short on weaner pigs though, several empty pens."

Mogford looked at the pigs. "When will you sell these?" he asked.

"About midday, I've got second turn today. Fraser's about to start. He has a new young man selling, and it looks a good entry."

"If you find some pigs in those empty pens they'll be mine," said Mogford, as he walked off to see the start of Fraser's sale.

The young auctioneer looked ill at ease, there were few buyers in attendance. He swung his bell valiantly. "Come along gentlemen," he called nervously. "I'm just about to start. A fine lot of pigs forward, come along, gather round." He put the bell down and started to sell.

"Who'll start me, five pounds apiece for this pen of fine weaner pigs. Five pounds I'm bid, any advance on five" . . . he caught Mogford's eye and noted the four fingers briefly exposed . . . "not a bid over there?" He looked in the opposite direction. "Then I have four pounds this side, four pounds I'm bid . . ."

With the small number of buyers unresponsive, and quickly realising that bids of five pounds were a fiction of the auctioneer's making, the prices remained low. The young auctioneer unwilling to end up with unsold pigs eagerly latched on to Mogford who at least was buying, albeit at his own price.

Mogford bought just enough to fill Pettit's empty pens. After Fraser's auction he moved his pigs down to Pettit's section, booked them in and went off to catch up on the gossip.

He visited the cattle pens to have a chat with Jimmy Wing's replacement. Jimmy had died a month before Christmas. Mogford had made sure that he had a decent and dignified send off. The local territorials provided a uniformed presence in honour of his war service, and the huntsman of the local pack stepped forward to blow 'gone away' over his grave.

The daughter, 'his little flower', went back to China. Mogford saw to the disposal of his lurcher and the ferrets and handed the key to his poor abode back to the landlord. Jimmy Wing had nothing of value; all he left behind was a memory of an eccentric figure, and a list of quotable expressions, 'come on m'dears, all together one at a time, right on there, one foot 'afore the other.'

Mogford heard a bell; that would be Pettit about to start. He made his way over to the pig pens where a sizeable crowd was already assembled. This was a better time of day to start selling. People with chores to do at home couldn't get in for an early start. By midday they had been in the market long enough to get jollied up.

Pettit was a popular auctioneer. He had a good line of patter; he knew his customers; there were 'in' jokes. He poked fun and got some back. The sale was going well.

Mogford climbed up beside Pettit on the plank over the pens; his recently acquired pigs were next.

"Come on folks, a nice lot of pigs in from Mr Mogford. I have to sell them a bit sharpish because he's in a hurry to get home to Martha. Start them at five fifty."

"Too high auctioneer," came a voice from the crowd.

"Don't worry Bert," called Mogford jovially. "They will be too dear for you."

"Us'll see about that Mogford," came back the voice, and the banter went to and fro', and Pettit with his lively delivery and a touch of showmanship, generated an excitement which resulted in good prices.

Mogford bustled off to pay his cheque to Fraser's office and collect a larger one from Pettit's establishment. He was well pleased with the balance.

That evening he said to Martha. "I do enjoy it m'dear but I feel I should be doing more. If for instance I got into exporting, Luke could travel, see a bit of the world, we would have a bit more money to set him up on his own one day."

"Then he could find a nice girl and settle down," suggested Martha.

"Well, I hadn't thought it through that far, I just wondered what you felt. You know I never take big risks, never more than I can get out of if it goes wrong. I would have to borrow and take bigger risks, but if it comes off, the rewards are bigger. What do you think?"

"I think you already have a scheme in your head, and you want to go on with it, and you just want my blessing. Well Mogford, I have faith in you, I'm behind you all the way. But," she added sharply, "you'd better be right."

A deal had been taking shape in Mogford's mind. A plan so big that it sometimes frightened him. But it was exciting; if he could pull it off; there was a lot of groundwork to do; it wouldn't happen right away, perhaps not before the summer.

"I heard a bit of gossip about that roadworks rumour in the market, m'dear," said Mogford. "I get the impression it's a big new road coming up past our village and going on towards the moors. Opening the place up a bit for tourists, and no doubt in time it will join up with a new main road. They're getting on with the motorways up country. It's only a matter of time before they come down here."

"At least it's not through our village," said Martha, "but where would it pass by?"

"I've thought about that," said Mogford. "There is only one sensible straight path. The village sits on a bend. If you draw a line past the village it goes straight across the cricket pitch."

"Oh, the vicar won't allow that, right through his

beloved cricket pitch. That would leave the church and the vicarage on the side of the main road. No I can't see that will come to pass somehow."

Mogford kept his counsel on that one, and Martha spoke again. "The summer bookings are coming in, I had a nice letter from Miss Pringle. She wants to book a week in August, and she wants to bring a friend."

Mogford groaned inwardly. Two of them this time he thought. Still perhaps they would keep each other out of mischief, chaperone each other, so to speak. Mogford could hardly have known what a grave miscalculation he was making about the friend.

* * *

Martha was always glad to see the back of that dreary time after Christmas and New Year and ready to welcome the spring. There was one little field alive with small wild daffodils, and the banks of the farm road were massed with primroses. Later a carpet of blue would spread itself among the trees in the wood. By then there might be a few paying guests.

She was looking forward to seeing Miss Pringle again in August. In a way it was a pity she was bringing a friend, but no, she mustn't go match making; still, she did like Miss Pringle. Luke could do worse. Martha was sure that behind the façade of reserve was a warm hearted loving person just waiting to be liberated.

"This time we'll try to get to the real Miss Pringle," she said out loud.

Hammy jerked into wakefulness, surprised at the suddenness and vehemence of the comment.

"And you will behave yourself this time my lad," she added grimly.

Hammy did not like the turn the conversation was taking, nor the tone of the voice; there was nothing about food or walkies. He went back to sleep. "Well at least we ought to get past the Miss Pringle bit, she must have a first name." Martha's final remark was directed at Hammy's unresponsive back.

Martha jerked her thoughts back to the present. Miss Pringle's visit was more than four months away. She should be thinking about Mogford's ploys, but that was difficult. He wasn't giving anything away at this stage.

But something was afoot. Mogford was more than usually furtive. There were many phone calls; some of them international. He had been down to the nearby RAF station more than once, and there were those phone calls from mysterious Welshmen. Luke was equally in the dark; all he knew was that Mogford had told him he would need that passport he had acquired for the South American trip. Martha was sure that the cards would be laid on the table soon. Most likely the breakfast table. And so it proved.

9
Big business

IN fact it was not until the middle of May that Mogford unveiled his plans.

As Martha had suspected, he laid his cards on the table one morning after breakfast.

It started out like any other morning. Hammy asleep by the Aga. Rip perched outside on the windowsill, watching Luke, with eyes alert, and ears pricking at any sign that he might be about to leave the table.

"The first consignment of Mogford calves will take off from the RAF runway round about the twentieth of June. You, Luke, will be on board, destination Italy." Mogford made his announcement with a fine sense of theatre.

Luke could only stare and Martha for once was lost for words, capable only of small gurgling noises.

Into this void Mogford poured the outline of his plan. "It's like this," he said. "There is a desperate need for veal calves in the Po Valley. That's in Italy . . . north Italy," he added for Luke's benefit. "At the same time there are surplus calves in Wales, not too far away. Many of these have been contracted for by operators of co-operative calf schemes who are desperately looking for markets. It seemed to me that someone ought to get them together. They need a middleman. I've been a middleman all my life. Now to the detail."

Martha was beginning to recover her voice. "But the regulations, export licences, veterinary . . ."

"I've been into all that," replied Mogford. "Veterinary was a bit tricky, what with Brucellosis about, but I've had talks; our premises are clean, one cow, and she's been tested clear. Only calves from accredited stock will come on the place. Some farmers are in voluntary schemes. Our veterinary people are happy enough to give me the green light. My contact man in Italy seems satisfied. The bank manager is happy. Now we have to make it happen. I have to firm up the orders and arrange deliveries. You Luke have to sort out the lairage."

"You're rushing on a bit Da'. What do you mean about lairage? Don't forget this is the first we've heard of it." Luke was recovering from the shock of Mogford's sudden revelation.

"Well you're the buildings man Luke, and these calves by law must have a place to rest – there are certain laid down standards – and be fed and watered before boarding the plane. I still have to finalise the charter plane and try to tie this up with the deliveries from Wales. Of course we may end up keeping the calves for a few days but there is plenty of leeway in the deal to cover that."

"Come on then Da', what must I do?"

Mogford was pleased with the way his family were taking it. "I'll leave that up to you Luke. It will mean some conversion of buildings, but we have space not being used." He beamed, "I hand that over to you. Of course you will go over with the calves. You could enjoy yourself over there."

"As long as he comes back," said Martha grimly. "I suppose your RAF chums are happy enough about you using the runway?"

"Happy as can be. I'm glad I always gave a good pig for their pig roast functions."

"Luke will need to spend on the old buildings," demurred Martha.

"It'll be a fairly quick turnover," replied Mogford, reassuringly, a few weeks at most, and there's a goodish margin for the middleman. Once we've been paid for the first load, we will knock a lump off the overdraft, and by the second, we will be showing a margin."

"It needn't cost the earth," offered Luke. "Some insulation; we might get away with kennels and natural ventilation. Ventilation will be important. We don't want the little beggars getting pneumonia."

"It seems a bit awful," said Martha, "transporting them so young."

"Well look at it this way m'dear. 'Bobby' calves don't have a bright future anyway. Often they're slaughtered out of the market at only a day or two. These will be a lot stronger than that and Luke and I will see to it that they have every comfort. Won't we Luke?"

"Right Da', as you say," Luke answered absently. His mind was already on plans; insulation, louvered vents, kennels and perhaps just a stray thought about landing for the first time in sunny Italy. He had heard that bottom pinching was a way of life. Funny goings on, but ... where there were bottoms there were girls.

Martha's thoughts were less sunny. The size of the proposed borrowing worried her. It would hang like a millstone round her neck. They had never borrowed before, and had always been able to weather a lean patch. What if something were to go wrong?

She felt Mogford's eyes on her; he was looking at her anxiously. "Try to look on the up side," he said gently. "This could set us up, build something worthwhile for Luke, I've got to do it m'dear. If I don't somebody else will."

Martha, despite her forebodings, had to agree.

* * *

The middle of June brought a mini heat wave. The beach was fairly busy. It amused Luke that with three miles of beach, people crowded up one end, near the café and the ice cream van.

Still it made his job easier. He surveyed the scene from his elevated chair. Luke was on lifeguard duty; weekend work he embraced in the season.

Luke felt good about himself. He was in fine shape, already taking on a nice tan, and he was not unaware of the odd sidelong glance from a pretty girl.

He had his eye on a small group of young things playing beach ball near his look-out post. Not too many were braving the sea. A few surfboarders in wet suits further along the beach; they could take care of themselves. Some youngsters with small boards were riding chest down on the breakers; they looked a bit chilly. The water was not too warm in June despite the hot sun; but they were safe enough, not venturing too far out.

Luke took his eyes off the beach game and scanned the sea. He had been watching a girl on a lilo earlier; not just because she had struck him as being rather attractive, but lilos were bad news, especially with an offshore breeze.

He had lost sight of her and he didn't think she had come ashore.

He spotted her about the same time that he became aware of an agitated couple running along the beach towards him.

She was too far out, she would soon be in danger, and she seemed to be peacefully dozing and unaware.

Luke paused only long enough to explain to the parents. "I'm going to run out on the headland. Hopefully I can get to the point before your daughter; I will get in the water there and tow her to land. Meantime though, to be on the safe side, phone RAF rescue . . ." and he was off running.

Luke had his second wind by the time he reached the point and slid into the water. He was behind the breakers, swimming in gentle swell. As he had anticipated the current had brought the lilo within thirty yards of the headland.

The girl opened her eyes as he put a hand on the air

bed. Luke grinned at her. "A bit far out for safety, your mum and dad are having kittens."

The girl sat up and looked around. She saw the distant shoreline in one direction and a grey expanse of open sea in the other. She turned wide eyes on Luke, and reached out to him with both hands.

The shift of weight was enough to release the unstable lilo from its supporting function. It bobbed out from under her and she was in the water clinging tightly to Luke.

Faced with a changed situation, Luke used his training to effect a competent rescue. A helicopter was overhead as they came ashore.

"Do you need a chopper?" asked Luke.

"No I'm fine, thanks to you," the girl smiled.

Luke waved the rescue helicopter away. "I don't have anything to put round you . . . except my arm, of course you're welcome to that," grinned Luke.

She smiled back. "I'm not really cold, but perhaps, just to steady me."

And so they arrived on the beach a little later. The parents showered Luke with their gratitude. "You must have dinner with us one evening, I'll call you," said the mother.

As they took their leave, the father handed Luke his card. It was a name well known locally and the address was impressive.

"It was the most competent and professional rescue," said he. "Of course we would have been much more worried but for the fact that Samantha is a very strong swimmer."

Luke thought he might hear no more, but in due course there was a telephone invitation to dine with the Fortescues at their country house.

Of course, he would go, even if it meant wearing a suit and tie and remembering his p's and q's at the Lord Lieutenant's table.

Samantha had been on his mind ever since the rescue. But *was* it a rescue. She was a strong swimmer, her dad had said so, she could have made it to the headland. But of course she was asleep, could have drifted for miles; that is if she really had been asleep. Luke thought he had detected a wicked twinkle in her eye as her father had revealed her swimming capability.

Yes, Luke thought, nothing would keep him away. He was attracted to Samantha as naturally as the lode-stone is to the magnetic pole. His father was always telling him. 'You have to be in the right place at the right time, and ready to grasp an opportunity when it sits up and looks at you.'

Well, this time, the place and the time had coincided, and if Samantha represented an opportunity, he was ready and willing. And he had no doubt his mother would be impressed.

* * *

While maintaining his usual, cheerful, unruffled outward demeanour, Mogford, if pressed, might have admitted to a certain disquiet about his present role of large scale entrepreneur.

Never before had he gone to his bank manager to ask for a large overdraft. True he had used the facility for small excursions into the red, but these were always short term and redeemable, even if on occasion it had meant a temporary tightening of belts.

This was different. The conversion of buildings had cost a pretty penny, despite Luke's clever use of secondhand.

He had contracted for enough calves for two plane loads, with options to purchase others, and the charter company had demanded deposits. Yes he was in up to the neck, and paying six per cent on everything he spent out.

Some instinct deep within him seemed to be crying out.

Mogford couldn't put his finger on it. He went over the logic of it time and again. It was a good deal, solid, well contracted for and liable to make him quite a bit. He couldn't really find a flaw. It was less risky than many of his small deals. It was protected all the way by contracts, signed and sealed. The only thing was, he had never dealt outside his own country before, in fact seldom outside his own area, and contracts were sealed by a slapping of hands. Somehow he felt he might have been happier if someone had slapped hands with him.

Anyway if this was big business, he was, as they say, in for a penny in for a pound. Some of the calves for the first load were already in the lairage, the rest would follow tomorrow, which was Tuesday, the flight was on Friday, and Mogford understood that his son had a dinner engagement on the Wednesday. Well, a proposed flight to Italy would be something to talk to the Lord Lieutenant about. He only hoped Luke wouldn't drink too much wine, burp, or tell unsuitable stories.

This of course was grossly underestimating his son. Luke, in pursuit of an objective could in his own way, play his cards as carefully as Mogford might, in coaxing a deal.

* * *

Despite a determination not to be overawed, Luke was a little nervous as he drove the family car up the long drive to the 'Hall'. The car was Luke's first concession to an upward movement in the social scale. Normally he did his courting in his van but Martha prevailed on him. The van wouldn't advance his cause, and besides it was rather muddy.

Like Mogford he was operating in uncharted waters. He would play it by ear.

The Queen's representative himself greeted Luke on the doorstep. Somehow he had expected a butler.

"Come in my boy, we've been looking forward to

meeting you again. Name's Bert by the way, call me Bert, no formality. Come inside, just family, me, Jemima my wife, and Sam. We're having a cocktail. Come inside."

Mrs Fortescue came forward and kissed him on the cheek. "Never miss a chance to kiss a hero. And he is our hero, isn't he Sam?"

"Of course he is," said Samantha coming forward in her turn and kissing Luke warmly on the cheek, but lower down; in fact just missing the corner of his mouth and lingering for that important second or two.

It was enough to make Luke's pulse race and his voice was a little unsteady when he spoke, "That dress you're wearing, it's . . . well . . . stunning. Must be a Paris model at least."

A flush of pleasure spread over Samantha's face. "What a lovely compliment. In fact I designed and made it myself. Well most of it. Mummy helped a bit with the sewing. That's what I want to do, dress designing. I send sketches off to the big fashion houses from time to time. So you see I'm just waiting to be discovered. I've done the college course, I want to get going in the real world."

"Do I call you Sam?" asked Luke quietly. They were standing a little apart from the parents.

"The family call me Sam, in fact most people do, but I want you to call me Samantha, to be different, to make it special."

Luke basked for a moment in a look from the dark eyes, that were soft, and full of promise. Just for a moment the mischief which made them dance, had gone. It was a look that spoke of love.

"Samantha it is," he said softly. "We can't do much with Luke to make it special."

"It's special enough," she said. "After all you saved my life."

"Hmm, I've wondered about that," said Luke. And that set her eyes dancing again, and they went in to dinner.

Bert Fortescue owned a small estate, with two farms,

some shooting and he headed up a firm of solicitors with branches in several towns. He had seen service in the army, retiring with the rank of colonel, and his main interests currently were Aberdeen Angus cows and Border Leicester sheep.

Luke was well able to hold up his end of the conversation on livestock and allied subjects but was a little surprised that it appeared Mrs Fortescue had cooked the meal and she and Samantha served it up. In fact not very different from a meal at home; good wholesome plainish food, except of course at home Samantha wouldn't be sitting across the table from him.

He was finding it hard to take his eyes off her. The girl in the wet swim suit with the bedraggled hair had been disturbing enough. The svelte girl in the gorgeous dress, which showed off creamy shoulders, smooth dark hair and laughing eyes was even more irresistible.

But his host was speaking again. "Do you ride old chap?"

"If you are talking about bicycles, yes I do," grinned Luke. "Horses no, I've never been on a horse."

"Well . . . horses in the stable here, eating their heads off. Sam would sort out a nice quiet nag . . . get you started."

"Great, I'd like that," Luke said with an enthusiasm which gratified his host.

"Good then," he said. "You and Sam can get together on the phone, sort something out. Might get the horses exercised."

As the meal progressed Luke warmed to this unpretentious family. The house could perhaps be described as a small manor, plainly furnished for the most part with what Luke took to be a few good antiques here and there. He knew the land was good and the sheep flock had a reputation for prolificacy even if there was an element of hobby about the Aberdeen Angus breeding herd. Horses in the stable were no great extravagance for an ex-cavalry man and there seemed to be little else of luxury on view. And then there was Samantha, sitting opposite, low cut at the neck, leaning forward slightly over her plate, meeting his eyes with charged glances as they exchanged commonplace items of conversation.

Luke left for home with his head in the clouds. Bumping about on horseback didn't appeal much, but he could learn. It wasn't too much to ask in the name of love. Perhaps they didn't need to ride very far; tether the horses, sit on the grass ... His mind on such flights of fancy, he hardly cared now about a bottom pinching expedition to Italy.

* * *

It was in the morning, in the shape of a letter from Italy that disaster struck. Luke's trip to Italy would have to be cancelled.

Pale faced and with a trembling hand Mogford passed the letter to Martha. "It's the worst possible news m'dear," he said. "It puts us in a poor position."

Martha took the letter and read it. "It's a bit late in the day for them to decide they can't take calves from a country which has brucellosis, even if the stock is tested free," she said indignantly. "We could be ruined."

"We've been let down," said Mogford. "Either our agent over there was unaware of the legislation, or had been given wrong advice about existing laws. Either way we're in the soup, good and proper. All the calves have been blood tested and given certificates. They are good clean stock but the home market's depressed, too many calves and too few buyers. We'd lose a packet."

"You mean," said Martha anxiously, "we might be in debt for a few years."

"Worse than that m'dear, we borrowed to convert the building, we part-paid the charter in advance. There's another load of calves contracted for. We have to take them, and every week these calves get bigger and eat more food. Whatever we do, I see us with a bank overdraft we can't repay; we then drop further and further behind."

"What if we fed the calves on, in the hope that the home market might improve?" suggested Luke.

"That's about all that's left to us," said Mogford wearily.

"Nobody wants these veal calves, but they might sell as young stores to beef feeders later on. It means I have to go cap in hand and beg for credit from our feed merchant. It buys us a bit of time. We might just cut our losses at some point. Meantime everything we spend costs us six per cent on top. The only real way out is to sell the farm."

"Oh Mogford, we can't let that happen, whatever would you do, whatever would any of us do? No there must be something we can try. We'll tighten our belts of course and I could go out and look for a job. We have to hang on as long as we can. These calves got us into this mess, they can get us out of it."

"Then you don't blame me, m'dear?"

Martha came and put an arm round Mogford.

"I was behind you in this Mogford," she said, "and I am behind you now that it's all gone wrong. Just don't you let it get you down. Carry on trading as you were. Luke will have his hands full looking after these calves. I will find some work. And," she added, "I know you scoff, but I shall find time for a little prayer."

"Maybe I was a bit greedy, bit off more than I could chew. Took too big a step upwards."

"You were exploiting a market situation. Buying cheap to sell dear. There's always going to be a risk when you take that first step. There's always somebody holding the poor cards. This time it's us, and we must buckle to. I shall need the car I'm going into town."

Martha spoke with a briskness she didn't feel. Indeed she was close to tears.

* * *

Martha approached the large red brick building with some trepidation. This was her third call, a large bakery complex, with a considerable need for labour in the season.

Her first two calls had been abortive. The town's prestigious hotel was fully staffed for the summer. Likewise at a restaurant which could make no use either of her cooking skills or her administrative talents.

This time she thought she would make no mention of her teaching qualifications.

The girl behind the enquiry window directed her to Personnel which turned out to be a small office staffed by one rather harassed looking man.

He motioned Martha to a seat and pulled a pad towards him.

"What have you got to offer?" he asked warily. "Skills, previous experience, references, etc."

"I am a farmer's wife and have a strong pair of hands," she said in a slightly aggressive way. "If that doesn't suit I can tell you more." She caught his eye and held it with a look that might have quelled a class years ago. Truth to tell she was a bit fed up after two rejections – and she needed a job. She noted with some satisfaction that the world weary man was now more alert and paying attention.

"Well that's a different attitude," smiled the man as he started to run his finger down a list.

"We get so many sent by the Labour Exchange who don't really want jobs. But I can see you do, help yourself to coffee – in the flask over there."

"Let's say I need a job," said Martha. She poured the coffee.

"One for you?"

"Thanks," he said and his finger hesitated. "No, that went yesterday."

Martha watched the moving finger till it had traversed several sheets and the man pushed the papers away.

"There is just one thing," he said. "Can you sew?"

Martha nodded, "I can sew, what is it? Have you lost a button?"

"It's a job," said the man. "All that's left, but it doesn't pay very well, in fact I hesitate to offer it, but an out-worker who made the hessian gloves for us has given up. The job is vacant, but it only pays pence per glove. Nobody, so far, has retired rich; it's a very poor rate per hour."

"I'll take it," said Martha. "Tell me more."

"Well, give it a try," said the man. "It solves a problem for me of course. I usually have to find a retired person. You know, with time to spare and a bit of other income. We supply an industrial sewing machine and the hessian and you can start right away."

"I have a car outside, I could take the hessian and a machine right away. And I would need a sample of the glove. What are they used for?" Martha stood up, well satisfied to have landed something, however un-promising.

"They are simple hessian mitts which the bakers slip on to handle the hot tins. Just show me your car and I will see to the loading. You might do a bit better than the others. After all," he smiled, "you are younger and you said yourself you have strong hands."

If Luke was surprised by the items he unloaded from the family car he did not show it.

"Are we going to make our own clothes Ma?" he enquired. "Sackcloth to go with the ashes?"

"This is no time for joking," snapped Martha. "This," she indicated the hessian and the machine, "is what they call slave labour. It's an area which the industrial revolution didn't reach. You will give a thought to mechanising the work."

Putting a part of his mind to work on his mother's production line Luke contemplated the interview he had arranged with Samantha's father. He had decided to put his pride in his pocket and ask for work on a part time basis. About three hours a day with an early start, was, he felt a possibility, especially as Mogford had declared he couldn't afford to take too many gambles in the markets. It was his intention to spend more time on the farm, take on some of Luke's work. After all there were all those extra calves.

* * *

Luke drove to the Hall in his van and wore his cords and a casual jacket. He was greeted courteously by the Lord Lieutenant.

"The thing is Mr Fortescue, I need to earn some money, my Da's in a bit of a hole," Luke came straight to the point.

"Sit down, do have a drink old chap, tell me all about it."

Bert Fortescue listened attentively as Luke gave an account of the Mogford's plight. He rubbed his chin as Luke finished.

"It's a brick wall," he said reflectively. "You're up against the foreign veterinary regulations. Head banging won't help. I'll give you some work."

"Not the horses," Luke said apprehensively.

"I'm afraid so, all we've got. Samantha has been doing it, but she really does work at her fashion drawings and needs more time for it. If you could get here at six, muck out, groom down and exercise. All done by nine. How about it?"

"Fine, I accept, but apart from mucking out, I will need to be shown."

Luke felt he could cope with the grooming, but the exercise, that was a bit drastic, he shared his father's fear of heights where horses were concerned. Still Samantha would be his mentor. That made up for a lot.

Luke had a natural affinity with animals and after about three days he had made friends and felt more comfortable with the horses. Exercise was still a bumpy business but he felt he was getting the hang of it. He looked forward to Samantha's morning tutorial even if she did sometimes approach the stable calling, 'Heathcliff, Heathcliff' in that silly voice. On such occasions he would amble to the stable door, tugging his forelock and calling her m'lady. He absolutely refused to roll in the hay with her during working hours, and he was a frequent guest at the Lord Lieutenant's dinner table.

Meals at the Hall were casual affairs with Luke invited to take pot luck, although Samantha contrived to appear in one of her creations from time to time. A stroll in the garden often followed where the conversation might be of roses, garden pests, farming and a host of other country subjects. The parents did not always elect to stroll and it was one perfect evening towards the middle of summer that Luke found himself alone with Samantha enjoying the stillness and warmth of the wall sheltered rose garden. The perfume of old fashioned roses was everywhere and birds were still twittering about their business. They strolled along a wide grass path, unhurried, hands interlocked, speaking seldom and quietly, in keeping with the gentleness of the fading day. At the end was an arbour where they kissed and clung.

"Do you think we're falling in love?" said Samantha softly.

"It feels like it," replied Luke. "I just know I want you. All of you, totally . . ."

"Body and soul. I know you want my body."

"Body and soul, all of you. But not here, not now, not in your parents' rose garden. It would seem like stealing."

"You mean if we could tell them something. Make an announcement it would be different?"

Luke nodded. "I suppose."

"Well, we'll sit for a spell, talk, kiss a little and walk back."

Darkness was dropping its veil and a moon was rising before they strolled back, hand in hand as before and talking softly.

10
Resolutions

THE production line at home was shaping up. Each evening found Luke in his workshop drilling, cutting, grinding and now he was ready for assembly. The barn was the only building long enough to house his invention. There was a Heath Robinson element to it as new materials had been out of the question. The roll of hessian was mounted on a spindle at one end. An old fashioned mangle, powered now by an electric motor, stood some way down the line. Between were arms set at declining angles. Beyond the mangle was a bench over which loomed a large guillotine knife fashioned by Luke from a scythe blade.

Luke was about to explain to his parents, who were recovering from the initial shock.

"I think I will demonstrate and explain as I go," he said. "You might be more convinced that way."

"We have every faith in you," said Martha doubtfully.

Luke grinned at this unenthusiastic vote of confidence and started by mounting the hessian on its spindle. He then unrolled the hessian as far as the mangle where he folded it and cranked it through by hand.

"All right so far?" he asked.

"I think I get it," said Mogford. "When you start up the old mangle it will unwind the roll and these metal arms are set at gradually reducing angles, so that it goes through the mangle folded.

"Right," said Luke. "The gloves have to be double thickness so we have taken care of that already."

"I knew we could rely on you Luke. What comes next?" enthused a now more convinced Martha.

"This is Da's area," replied Luke. "The mangle will drop the doubled hessian in folds. You Da' will pull the end of the piece down the bench to the guillotine. There's a line marked on the bench, this gives the width of the glove. You need one hand to operate the tackle, the other arranges the hessian. This has one great advantage." He paused for effect. "You are only likely to lose the fingers off one hand."

"Thanks," said his father drily. "But I can see it could be very quick. Tug – thump – tug – thump. As quick as that."

"Quite," said Luke. "Like any good production line, we put pressure on each other. The faster you cut, the quicker goes Ma who's sewing, here, right next to you, and the more she sews the more I have to turn right side out. And of course, I shall bundle up in twelves. We can then measure our work at two shillings a bundle. What do you think?"

"I think we should start up and have a go. It looks good, Luke." Mogford turned to Martha. "And you m'dear have made it all possible. What a family to have around in a crisis."

"The old mangle," said Luke. "Well she was never designed for speed work. I have geared her to go at a fair lick. That puts pressure on you Da'. She might rattle a bit but I have packed the old lady thick with cart grease."

"We can wear ear muffs if necessary. Come on Mogford, let's get to our stations. Go on Luke, start her up." Martha was firmly of the opinion that work was good for the soul.

Indeed they all felt better after an evening of trouble free production, and a satisfactory number of two shilling bundles in the despatch area.

* * *

Time passed, and Mogford became more grey faced and anxious with each passing day. He did his sums endlessly. Martha's initiative, and Luke's earnings, were a help, but could only slow the downward slide. Mogford could see them sinking, slowly, but inevitably into a situation where the only solution would be the sale of the farm. He had felt an instinctive sense of foreboding when he had pledged the deeds to the bank against his borrowing. The deeds had never been so used before, not by himself, not by his father, he felt like a traitor, a betrayer of his family past and present, a failure. He had lost money before on deals that went wrong. That was all part of the cut and thrust of dealing. The family had sometimes had a lean patch while they got over it, but the farm, their home, had always been safe, a citadel, from within which the family could repel invaders.

But now there was no fortress it was guerilla warfare with the odds against them stacked high.

Soon the calves would be eating quantities of solid food. The merchant would carry him; but for how long? The bank would be unhappy about a large and solid overdraft, how long before the bank manager started to worry?

Mogford knew he needed a miracle and he knew exactly what form that miracle must take. He explained all this to Luke.

"What we need Luke is a dramatic rise in price when the calves are weaned on to solid food. Not just a rise to normal market levels but considerably above. We have to take delivery of another lot of calves which were contracted for. We can't hold them off much longer. With the numbers we have to sell we could just about get out."

"We do need a miracle then," said Luke. "There doesn't seem any way that prices will get up. They are solid rock bottom now."

Martha contributed a comment. "Miracles sometimes do happen," but even she didn't expect one.

Martha was washing dishes one day when she thought of the large up-country dealer who had helped her to buy her calves in the local market. It was not the only time she had given him a thought. It had been such a lovely day. He had taken her to tea. Made a fuss of her. Yes, her thoughts had lingered pleasantly over the day on more than one occasion, but this time it was different, she was thinking business. He was up-country, he was at the heart of things, and he was an important dealer. He had an organisation. He and his friends could influence prices. It was worth a try.

She found his card in a deep part of her handbag. Hamish Mackay, etc., etc., and a telephone number. She reached for the telephone. She made no bones about it.

"Hamish we're in desperate trouble. We need help." Martha explained in detail and Hamish listened.

When she had finished Hamish said, "Martha dear, if I could help, you know I would, but the market is just as depressed up here, even more so. If you are forced to sell I could probably make a better price than most, but I wouldn't want that. I'll keep an ear to the ground. If anything changes I'll be in touch." He talked a little longer but it was clear to Martha that he had nothing to offer.

Martha put the phone down and pondered on his final piece of advice. 'I would hang on to the bitter end, something might change. We might be having tea together one day and laughing about all this.'

Martha didn't feel much like laughing at that moment. It worried her that Mogford was so changed. He had become a serious, hard working man, at his best working at top speed on the production line, or labouring on the farm. He was no longer doing deals in the market. She missed the effervescent, confident little dealer who never missed a trick, the bubbling, twinkling, rotund husband so full of fun, so full of optimism.

Martha knew full well that if anyone was going to find a way out of their difficulties, it would be Mogford. But the old Mogford, not the serious, worried man she now shared her life with. This man who endlessly worked on his figures, who pored over the papers of the aborted deal. Two contracts signed and sealed; two plane loads already paid for, and other contracts already signed by the co-operatives, anxious to sell, and just needing Mogford's signature to ensure a plane load per month for the next twelve months.

Martha had to agree it had been a well set up deal; but how unhealthy for Mogford to be so preoccupied with it; it was a dead thing, in the past. And those Ministry leaflets, how many more must he read, farming magazines as well. Always reading, studying, phoning the Ministry for more leaflets. Yes, Martha was worried about what was happening to Mogford.

* * *

Luke was a much improved rider. Ninety per cent of the time he rose correctly. He had soon learned that coming down when the horse was going up was a spine jarring and painful experience. He had enjoyed the job, at first, because of Samantha's morning visit, and the times when she would ride out with him to exercise the horses. Now he was beginning to appreciate the job for itself. He was becoming fond of the horses, and enjoyed looking after them. The shine on their coats was reward in itself, but of course, the extra cash was handy at home.

The calves were now being described as strong weaners and the trade hadn't improved.

Luke was putting a final shine on the horses with a piece of velvet one morning when he heard a familiar call.

"Heathcliff . . . Heathcliff . . ."

He responded with his usual shambling walk. "Marnin' m'lady," he mouthed. "Ee do looks purty this marnin'. Ah could fain kiss y'r 'and." He suited his actions to his words. "And your eyes, those little ear lobes, your sweet mouth, the slender pillar of your neck."

"Come up for air, do," gasped Samantha. "We're going riding, we won't go far. Come on let's saddle up."

"Exercise?" queried Luke.

"No we're not leading any horses today. Just you and I, riding out into the country. We'll tether the horses and sit under a tree."

"I've often pictured it like that, just the two of us, under a tree, the horses grazing nearby, you making a daisy chain, but of course, not in working hours." Luke grinned. "Perhaps I can stretch a point today."

"Perhaps you should, my darling," said Samantha, suddenly serious. "I have something to say to you. I don't think you're going to like it."

* * *

Martha was washing eggs when Luke got home. "Who stole *your* scone?" she demanded briskly. "You look about as miserable as your father is these days. Come on, sit down, I'll make you a cup of coffee."

"Where is Da'?" asked Luke.

"Oh he had some letters to post. He went off with some big brown envelopes. I don't know what he's up to. If he's not reading leaflets he's talking to the Ministry people about this scheme and that scheme. I wish I thought he had a trick up his sleeve, but I doubt it. No, this has fair knocked him out."

"Maybe you shouldn't count him out just yet. I've known boxers get nearly counted out and get up off the canvas to win with one big hit. Da' might just have one big punch left."

"Well, he might have," said Martha doubtfully. "I just think he's feeling too low to throw it. It's the thought of losing the farm, that's what's done it. Come to that you're looking a bit down yourself. What have *you* lost?"

"Samantha," said Luke simply. "I've lost Samantha."

"Oh dear." Martha handed him a cup of coffee. "Oh Luke I'm sorry to hear it. You too – well I thought you were getting serious. But come on – sit down, tell me all about it, it helps to talk to someone, even your old mother. What happened?"

"She's going to America. A position in some fashion house. Some Americans over here, saw a sample of her work in a London dress design place where she was known. They have offered her a position with prospects. She'll climb, be a big success, she has talent. She says she'll be back but I doubt it."

"Her career means a lot to her, doesn't it Luke?" said Martha gently. "You always knew that."

Luke nodded. "Yes I always knew she wanted to make a success of her design work, and it would have been a waste not to develop that talent. Perhaps I just didn't guess how strong that need was."

"Well don't wear your heart on your sleeve, there's more fish in the sea . . ."

"Yes I know Ma, than ever came out of it. I've heard that one before, and I always took that view. This time though, I was getting silly ideas, about settling down, children, you know – getting married."

"There's nothing silly about that. It's time you were settling down, although," she paused to reflect "your father didn't settle down that young, and I think he scattered a few wild oats along the way."

Luke felt better for having talked to his mother. The Citadel hadn't quite broken down. There was still strength within the family. If only his father would sit down and talk *his* worries through. He had become so furtive; spending time in his cubby-hole of an office, quiet, withdrawn. If only he'd spin a yarn, crack a joke, laugh a little.

For himself, he was sure he would never laugh again, and the ache in his heart would be there forever.

* * *

A week later details of a compulsory scheme to eradicate brucellosis were circulated. It was to be effected on an area by area basis. Mogford was already well informed and could quote clause by clause from memory.

Then there was a telephone call from Hamish Mackay. "I'm going to need some of those wee calves you've been keeping Mogford," he said.

"They're not wee calves any longer," replied Mogford. "More like strong stores and a bit pricey. I expect people are beginning to slaughter out up country?"

"Well a few are," admitted Hamish cautiously.

Mogford laughed. Martha and Luke started at the sound. Even Hammy raised his head.

"The Lord be thanked," said Martha fervently.

"More to do with the brucellosis scheme," whispered Luke.

Mogford was talking again. "If you want to get in on the ground floor, come and see me. I can offer you some right off, and more every month for a year. Luckily I signed all the contracts I had waiting for my signature, prices, delivery dates, and all from accredited sources, you know, people in voluntary schemes, and I was able to change a fair number to heifer calves. I've got the stock you've got the outlets. If you want a deal slap the phone your end and I'll do the same, it's the nearest we can get to a hand slap. Get down here tomorrow and we'll talk about contracts." There was the sound of a slap and Mogford came in to the room.

"That opportunity paid the penalty for sitting up and looking at you Da'," observed Luke.

Martha just held out her arms. Luke went outside. It was too painful; the spectacle of his father sobbing in his mother's arms was having an effect on his own composure. He found a quiet corner and shed a few tears of his own.

* * *

Luke was on his high seat surveying the beach with a jaundiced eye. Out there somewhere was America.

He felt like getting in the water and swimming in that general direction till exhaustion took over and he could sink to the depths. He cast a disinterested eye over the girls having fun and games around his perch. He noted with clinical detachment that one slender body in a bright red two piece, was pleasing to the eye. She was lightly tanned, and a bright lively face was topped by a mass of corn coloured curls. She seemed to be giving him the eye, so he smiled back mechanically, before turning to view the sea and resume his brooding thoughts. Young girls were so tiresome he thought. Getting into huddles, whispering and giggling.

He looked down again as the scrum broke up and the girls headed for the surf. Thank goodness, that'll keep them out of the way for a bit he thought sourly. His call to duty came five minutes later. The girls in the surf were calling and pointing. Further out he caught a flash of red and a hand raised, before the water closed over, and there was nothing.

Luke pinpointed the spot. He churned through the surf, diving under the waves, and came to the relative calm beyond. A sigh of relief escaped him as he saw the raised hand. Then down she went again. The second, the third time. He was on the spot and diving. There she was, just below the surface floating limply.

Well, dead or alive he must get her ashore. Turning her unresisting body on its back he headed for the shore.

On the beach he stretched her out and got astride to pump water. It was at that moment that she turned over, opened her eyes and smiled. "You were terrific," she said in a surprisingly strong voice. I'm O.K. really. I didn't swallow any water. Perhaps if you could help me up and just hold me a little."

"Well," as he explained to his mother later. "It's the least you can do when someone's had a bad experience."

What he didn't tell his mother, was how her wet golden curls came just below his chin and how as he helped her into her towelling wrap a little later, she reached in a pocket and handed him a slip of paper.

"My telephone number in case you should need it," was what she said.

Not, of course, that in his situation he would use it. Well maybe not right away . . .

And what was that his mother was muttering as she walked away. 'More fish in the sea . . .'

11
In the name of progress

THE vicar was the first to spot the red and white surveyor's poles making a straight line across the cricket field. It brought him closer to blaspheming out loud than anything since that time he had stopped a cricket ball with his unguarded shin. As it was, his lips moved as he strode out to make sure he wasn't seeing things.

No, his eyes had not deceived him. A Mogford sheep was rubbing itself against one of the offending objects. A man at the end of the field was gesticulating and shouting bad words at the sheep, alternating this with squints through a surveyor's level. Another man was obviously charged with the task of tapping in poles under direction from his partner in crime.

The vicar bore down on the man with the level, scattering red and white poles as he went.

"I won't allow it. I tell you, I won't have it. Get off my cricket field."

At one time the vicar's voice would have filled a cathedral. Now, in old age, it had climbed a few octaves and had a quaver in it, both peculiarities accentuated by rage. The qualities that had survived, were volume, and a fast delivery.

The torrent poured at and around the unfortunate man. He looked around swiftly for an escape route. Had a tree been to hand he might have shinned up it. As it was he had to attempt a defence.

An attack of splutters from the vicar allowed him to open his case. "We have permission. Only a preliminary survey. Choice of three routes. Might not happen." The man spoke in shorthand, partly to make maximum use of what promised to be a short lull, and partly because he was rather unnerved. He was unaccustomed to dealing with vicars and certainly not irate ones. His vocabulary, fine for sheep and work mates, was totally unsuited to a debate with a reverend.

It took time to convince the vicar that the end of the world was not nigh, and that there would be ample opportunity to view routes and lodge objections, arrange protest meetings, lobby MPs and generally create chaos.

Somewhat mollified by the amount of anarchy in which he could play a leading role, the vicar set off across the pitch to seek out Blackie. As he went he kicked over any poles which remained standing.

He found Blackie lovingly doing maintenance work on his cider press. It was only July, plenty of time yet, but if Blackie wasn't actually making cider, or drinking it, he was preparing to make it, or drink it.

The vicar waved away the offer of a taster from a discoloured horn receptacle. Blackie promptly despatched the sample, to save pouring it back.

"I shall call a public meeting," quavered the vicar, still on fairly high volume. "I shall make an announcement from the pulpit on Sunday."

"Hmm, that'll only get the message to about six old ladies Vicar, hardly spreadin' the message far and wide." Blackie grinned. "It a'nt no good us goin' off the deep end about this 'ere. I is as upset about it as you be, but us must go steady, step by step, make a plan; I'll spread the word in the pub, that'll get to most of the village, an' I'll talk to Mogford."

"Mogford," repeated the vicar. "Yes we must get Mogford involved. He's bound to know somebody on the Council, pull a few strings, wheels within wheels . . ."

"Steady on Vicar," interrupted Blackie. "Us don't want to get devious. Leave the devil's work to the devil. Mogford be a good man to 'ave on our side. Ee can play a straight bat, so to speak, but ee do 'ave a few tricky shots in his locker, an' ee do 'ave the good o' the village close to 'is 'eart. Ee won't be too keen on losin' a bit o' cheap grazing neither."

"I feel so angry, it's so unfair, this country's turning into a dictatorship, no democracy." The vicar was beginning to wind up again, "I will lie down before the bulldozers. It'll be over my dead body . . ."

"Steady now Vicar. Woah, back up there. Your dead body a'nt goin' to serve us none. Don't ee forget that we had a 'alf promise from the County to come down next season."

The vicar brightened up perceptibly. "Oh I do hope they can come. It's been a lifetime ambition to play cricket with class players. It would be a fitting climax . . . I might even retire after that."

"Retire!" Blackie was caught wrong footed. "I thought you'd never . . . well anyway it war that book o' Bob's what made us a bit famous for a day or two. Photos in the paper, tele. Well if County do come next season, it'll 'elp Bob's book sales an' o' course us might get a few folk come to watch."

"Could mean a very substantial collection," said the vicar, his voice perhaps ever so slightly tinged with envy. He knew almost to a penny what he could expect from his six little old ladies in church on Sunday.

A meeting was to be held in the village hall the following Wednesday. Mogford was informed by Blackie, who felt the occasion was important enough for a personal visit rather than a telephone call.

"The Vicar be up to high doh 'bout this un," said Blackie. "As a disaster ee do put it alongside of the flood or the black plague, but us needs somebody outside of cricket to look straight at un. It a'nt just the cricket team, it be the whole village. I be proper upset 'bout it but there be two sides to everything. You remember Mogford, when tractors came in an' they liddle ole horses went off the farms. My smiddy 'ad to close, but then there war more time for cider makin'."

When he left, he placed a small jar of his special brew on the kitchen table.

"I'll put it under the stairs," said Martha.

"If you think it's safe," grinned Mogford. "It's definitely not for drinking. It might come in handy as embrocation some time."

"Blackie's right though," said Martha. "There are two sides to this road business. The road through the village is narrow, not much more than a lane, and there's a fair bit of traffic in the summer; holiday people heading for the moors."

"Not too safe for children," agreed Mogford. "But on the other hand the traffic would rush on past on the new road, without hardly knowing the village exists. The village shop would miss the passing trade, and the pub; they let a couple of rooms, and there's the B and B people."

"They say there's a choice of routes, maybe the cricket field could escape," suggested Martha.

Mogford shook his head. "Just think about it m'dear. It's the only straight line and it's level. There's nothing to touch it for cost effectiveness. The alternatives are only to give a semblance of democracy."

"And there's land acquisition," said Martha. "Who owns the land now? I know it used to belong to the old Club President."

"A nephew," replied Mogford. "He inherited. An absent landlord. I should think he'd sell, and if not, they'll soon clap a compulsory purchase order on it. No m'dear we'll lose the ground sooner or later. Compromise that's what it'll come to. Not everyone can win; but we don't want winners and losers. In the meantime m'dear there will be bad blood in the village over this, and I shouldn't wonder if it doesn't start at this open meeting."

And start it did. The vicar and Blackie were on the platform. Blackie still moderate in his views, roseate of complexion, teeth flashing smiles under his heavy black moustache, feeling well disposed towards his fellow men. The vicar strident in his opening address and blinkered to the effect he was having on the villagers, was tending to the dramatic. "I shall lay down before the bulldozers," he shrilled. "They take the field over my dead body."

"It 'ud save the grave digger a job any road," a stout lady retorted.

"That was uncalled for Mrs May." The vicar recognised one of his congregation. She lived in the village and had a B and B sign outside her house.

Blackie in his role as chairman, called for quiet, and addressed himself to Mrs May. "Now m'dear, if ee ha' ort to say let's 'ave it."

Mrs May made the point that the cricket field route was hard by the village, and with adequate signs on the main road, visitors might divert to shop or more importantly, stop over in B & B. The other routes were miles away and represented ruin and destitution to anyone trying to turn an honest penny from tourists.

Blackie nodded sagely and said, 'Good point' several times.

The vicar spluttered and became pop eyed and rather pink.

The chairman was less moderate when someone pointed out the irrelevance of having a cricket team. This individual seemed to have an encyclopaedic knowledge of results over a number of years.

There was little need to remind Blackie of last year's results. One win and one match drawn. That was the time it rained all day and both sides repaired to the pub and got drunk behind closed doors. It was when the speaker became personal that Blackie took umbrage. Perhaps the vicar *was* too old, and losing his sight. He himself would be the first to admit that his own obesity did nothing for his game.

Blackie did not let the protester get further down the list before he invited him outside to settle things at the back of the hall.

The man looked at Blackie, on his feet now and no longer genial. He declined the invitation, and said he was ready to apologise and would withdraw the remarks.

Mogford unobtrusive in the body of the hall, made notes which he studied later with Martha.

"It seems to me m'dear," he said, "that the village has accepted that the road will come. It's a question of where. The folk who want tourists to come to the village and stay over or spend some money, are for the cricket field route. The others, mainly the cricketers, want a route that takes tourists well away from the village and spares the ground, such as it is."

"Well we can't have people falling out," said Martha firmly. "You'll just have to do something Mogford."

"I might possibly have a glimmer," said Mogford.

Martha was pleased to see the twinkle back in his eyes.

Mogford went on. "It might take some time, and people will fall out in the meantime. Things have a way of getting worse before they get better." He smiled. "I have some thinking to do."

* * *

Martha was relaxing with a cup of coffee and a biscuit after a busy couple of hours preparing rooms for Miss Pringle and her friend. It was a bit different in my day, she mused; two single rooms; Miss Pringle had been quite specific about that. Well perhaps they were a bit better off nowadays. In her young days they would have shared to save the pennies.

Hammy was sitting up and alert. He was well aware of

course, of the rule, 'no feeding between meals, the old devil will get too fat,' but Martha was nibbling biscuits. There was always the chance she might drop a crumb or two or even in an absentminded moment, offer him one. Martha was addressing him now directly. He must put his head to one side.

"Funny how things have worked out. Not so many weeks ago Mogford was in the pit of despair. Now he's fizzing and popping like a fire cracker. Take that business of the calves."

Hammy indicated a willingness to take that business, by gently flicking the tip of his tail. He also took the biscuit which Martha absentmindedly proffered, delicately extracting it from her extended fingers.

"That was a nightmare, the sword of Damocles hanging over us. I think to claim divine intervention might be too much, but something made me phone Hamish McKay, and that was a help at least. You know, Hamish was so impressed with Mogford; the way he kept up with events, and pulled off that deal with the co-operatives even though he was on the floor, knocked out, beaten, done for; that he tried ever so hard to get Mogford to join him, be a director, take over the south west area. But not Mogford; much too independent for that. Still he was happy to co-operate, and the business is going well and Hamish suggested we might have tea together when he is next down our way."

Martha's laugh tinkled happily. Hammy stood up and wagged his tail uncontrollably. It was a wag that started halfway along his back and culminated in tail sweeps in all directions. Hammy was pleased to hear laughter in the house, and fun, and banter. There had been a period of gloom and quiet. But Martha had not quite finished.

"And then there was that second meeting of the village folk about the road. Mogford prevailed on the meeting to appoint a small committee of people without a vested interest to sort out the best way forward. And who better than Bob, Percy Percival and Mogford to do just that."

Hammy had settled down for a nap and Martha had just got around to thinking what Bob's book had done for the village cricket team – local television, articles in the press, magazine features – when the sound of wheels bumping down the farm lane announced the imminent arrival of Miss Pringle and friend.

Martha had time only for a quick recap on the arrangements – flowers in the rooms, clean towels in the bathroom, kettle simmering on the Aga – before it was time to open the door and greet her guests.

12

Miss Pringle and friend

AND there they stood. Miss Pringle without glasses, hair fluffing out attractively, looking neat in her holiday clothes, short denim skirt, bare brown legs, smiling with pleasure, her hand tucked affectionately under her companion's arm.

"This is Clifford," she said, drawing the young man forward.

Martha stopped herself from exclaiming, 'a man' and instead held out her hand and said, "Pleased to meet you Clifford." Not for a moment had she expected Miss Pringle to produce a man friend. A chum, a gym mistress, the French mistress, somehow she had not bargained for a male of the species.

"Come inside, the kettle's on the boil. We'll get the luggage in a minute," and Martha was recovering from her surprise and being the good hostess, which was second nature to her.

As she conducted them to their separate rooms, she had a little inward chuckle. Luke was in for a surprise, and Mogford would be pleased. It didn't suit her book though. Not one little bit.

Miss Pringle, the old hand, was showing Clifford round the farm when the men arrived to prepare for supper.

Luke was the first to recover from Martha's news. "Darn it, and I was looking forward to taking Betty to the

Young Farmers' Club barn dance. It is to be a square dance, you know, denims, straw hats and check shirts, do-si-do and swing your woman, applejack, banjos and fiddles, dirndl skirts, a real feet stomping rave up, what a pity."

"Betty," said Mogford "you called her Betty I never knew her first name."

"Me neither." Martha admitted.

"Oh, I always called her Betty, in private . . . the last time . . . you know."

"Well I think you ought to take Betty *and* Clifford, to the barn dance. It's the least you can do. Help to make their holiday, so to speak. When is it?" Martha liked her guests, to have every opportunity to sample whatever entertainment was available.

"Friday night. They leave on the Saturday, don't they? Why not. Give them a good send off. Right, they're on if they want to go." Luke leapt to his feet as Miss Pringle ushered Clifford into the kitchen. "Just making plans for you," he said, shaking hands and kissing her lightly on the cheek. He gave Clifford a hand shake which made him wince. "Barn dance, American style, dress up, dirndl skirt, dungarees, red braces, corn cob pipe, what you fancy, what do you think?"

"I think I'd like to come. What do you say Clifford?"

Luke noticed with satisfaction how her eyes lit up with excitement at the prospect. "Clifford?" she asked again.

Clifford shrugged. "Righto Betty, if that's what you want to do."

During supper Luke found his eyes straying in the direction of Miss Pringle or Betty as everyone was now calling her. She really was attractive. Without her glasses there was a quality about her which Luke found appealing. He liked the fluffed out hair, and her face, so expressive now, with no hint of primness, and those nice tanned legs. What she saw in that Clifford he couldn't imagine. Perhaps a great brain lurked behind those thick horn rimmed glasses. Whatever hidden qualities he possessed, remained under wraps during the meal. He made little or no conversation. Betty on the other hand was quite animated, and Luke benefiting from recent, elevated, social contact, was able to conduct himself with an easy confidence.

"Did you see anything of interest round the farm?" Mogford directed his question at Clifford.

"In fact, yes," replied Clifford seriously. "Some excellent examples of dung fly on the dung hill, and I saw a pig louse for the first time, and of course there were quite a few common house flies and others around the cow."

"Clifford's something of an entomologist," explained Betty. "I hope that pig louse wasn't on that fine boar Romanoff. Do you still have him Luke?"

"Afraid not," said Luke. "Died pleasantly from overwork."

Mogford was sure Luke had flashed a quick wink at Betty and got a flicker back. An element of danger still lurked. Mogford could have wished that Clifford had some of the qualities of a John Wayne or a Gregory Peck. He would be no match for the muscular, physical presence of their Luke. Still she seemed fond of this owlish serious boffin, protective of him, and making up to him quite a bit when Luke was around. She seemed to be giving Luke the odd signal. Funny creatures women.

Was she, Mogford wondered, playing it from both ends. Using Clifford to make Luke keener, or perhaps using Luke to stir the other young man out of his preoccupation with insects; show him the way so to speak. Mogford decided he must await developments.

Betty with the experiences of other visits to call on, was keen to show Clifford her agricultural expertise. She demonstrated how to milk Daisy, who was feeling benevolent enough to part with half a bucketful of milk, before Clifford was prevailed on to take the stool.

Tugging fruitlessly, he engaged Martha, who was

hovering round the operation, on the life cycle of the warble fly.

Daisy, by this time was becoming weary of amateurs and put a stop to things by placing a hoof in the bucket.

The visitors were content, it seemed, to spend part of the day round the farm with Luke. Conflict sometimes arose when Betty might suggest a visit to the beach and Clifford would have preferred a visit to the abattoir where there might be the chance of seeing liver fluke, round worms, milk spots on livers, and all sorts of fascinating things; or he may have spotted a rare species of butterfly, or found some fascinating new pattern in the behaviour of wood lice. Mogford from his observations decided that Luke had the inside track, and he had to admit to himself that Betty was a much better prospect than the Miss Pringle of previous visits. Martha had been impressed by the way she had sat down and pulled half a pail of milk from Daisy. Daisy was inclined to resent strangers and hold back her milk. And then there was a spunky attitude over the new road. She had to be restrained from organising a placard protest outside the council offices. 'Hands off our village'. 'Save the cricket field'.

Mogford had to admit she was acquitting herself with a great deal of credit. And of course Martha liked her and so did old Hammy, and Luke's eyes kept straying in her direction. Yes things were building up. Perhaps the dance would bring things to a head. Whichever way the cat should jump, Mogford felt powerless to stop it. Strong feelings were building; an atmosphere; it was like watching a thunderstorm build, waiting for the strike of lightning and the roll of thunder.

Well there would be three of them, nothing much could happen. A good 'ho down' might relieve the tension. No, for an upcountry girl she was not a bad sort. When she came again he might take her to the market.

* * *

Betty went shopping on the Friday, and in the evening when she came downstairs wearing her purchases, Luke was surprised into a gasp of pleasure.

She was perfect. The flared skirt would twirl, the light tan boots would pass for cowgirl footwear, the check shirt, the neckerchief, and the waistcoat, topped off with a fluff of blonde hair and a face which mirrored the excitement within.

Clifford had made one concession to the occasion, he wore a bootlace tie.

Luke himself, as befits one who would share the task of 'calling', wore his best jeans and a check shirt. "Give us a twirl then," he said.

Betty twirled demurely.

"Perfect," said Luke. "You look really lovely."

Betty flushed with pleasure. "We've never done square dancing before have we Clifford?"

"I've never done any kind of dancing before," said Clifford glumly.

Luke grinned. "I'll see you through it. Half the people will be learners. Just listen to the caller."

Martha gave Betty a quick hug. "You just enjoy yourself my dear. Let your hair down and you could be the belle of the ball. You look lovely, doesn't she Luke?"

"Yes Ma' I'll be proud to escort her, er . . . them both to the shindig." He loosed off a fearsome cowboy 'ya-hoo'. "Come on let's go, the buggy is at the door. Oh! I've put a bale of straw in the back for you to sit on Clifford. Sorry about that, I'm not too well equipped for threesomes."

The dance was being held on a farm just the other side of the village. Luke knew that Betty had been looking forward to meeting some of the locals. They would all be there, if not for the dancing, then to help out with the applejack.

The farm yard had been swept clean. Old farm wagons and implements, relics of the horse drawn days, had been dragged from the nettles on various farms to give a flavour of the old West. Stable lanterns hung from vantage points, and three bored looking horses, hitched in time honoured way to a rail, gave testimony to how some had travelled.

As they approached the large double doors of the barn, Luke felt Betty's hand creep timidly under his arm. As he pulled it more firmly into place he noticed a slight tremor.

"Are you cold?" he asked.

"No, just nervous," she replied.

"Don't worry," Luke now had his arm round her shoulders, holding her close to him. "I'll look after you; although I shall have to do some 'calling' later on. But you have Clifford and I'll introduce you around. Just relax, you had your orders from my Ma', let your hair down, have a good time."

Then they were inside, and someone was handing them glasses of applejack, and they were part of the jostling, laughing throng.

"Howdy folks," a voice boomed behind Luke and his friends. They turned to confront Blackie's large and jovial presence. "Pretty poor stuff, this 'ere applejack. Just watered down cider I reck'ns."

Luke grinned. "Not up to your standard, pretty harmless I would say, anyway meet my friends, Clifford and Betty."

Blackie advanced on Betty and enclosed her slim hand in two hands the size of soup plates. "Ee is a really pretty liddle ole maid, sure 'nuff. That there Luke is a lucky young feller."

"Oh, Betty's with Clifford really," cut in Luke hastily. "I'm er . . . with both of them."

"Well ee could 'ave fooled me," said Blackie, reluctantly releasing Betty's hand. "If ee should want to taste a drop o' real cider I 'ave a bit wi' me. Just a sample like."

Luke held up his hands. "No Blackie, thanks, we'll make do with the weak stuff."

And then the music swept Luke and Betty into a dance. Blackie turned to someone else to complain about the applejack, and Clifford looked for a quiet corner where he could be alone with his thoughts.

Betty had plenty of partners. Luke's friends in the Young Farmers' Club were attentive. Betty was vivacious, and mingling with the villagers. Blackie could be seen on occasion escorting her, large hand decorously on elbow, making introductions, helping her to applejack.

Luke, now engaged in calling, could no longer attend her, and indeed it seemed, she was more than able to look after herself. He was aware of a feeling, not one he was used to, was it pique, or was it perhaps a twinge of jealousy? Still he was pleased she was having a nice time.

It was some time later when he caught a glimpse of Blackie, at the end of the barn, reaching into a crack between two bales to produce a pitcher, that he started to worry, for seated on one side of him was Betty and on the other was Clifford. Then the dancers swirled across his line of vision and he had to concentrate on the job in hand, and the incident slipped his mind.

He was reminded of it forcibly, some minutes later. He groaned. Of course Betty would want to try the 'real stuff', he should have warned her, but now it was too late.

Betty and Blackie were occupying the far corner of the floor. They were dancing, not following the caller but improvising wildly, Betty spinning and twisting like a dervish. Blackie, not designed by nature for dancing, had nevertheless a gift for theatre, and made up for a lack of suppleness and lightness of foot with rhythmic foot stomping, body shaking, and facial grimaces. The spectacle was so arresting that, couple by couple, the other dancers stopped to watch.

Luke pushed through the crowd. "Oh my God," he groaned.

Betty was dancing with the abandonment of an Isadora Duncan her full skirt flying waist high as she twirled.

Young Farmers were whistling their appreciation. Blackie stomping, knees bent, bottom and chest pushed out, fingers snapping, was being cheered for his elephantine contribution.

Luck sent the dervish careering towards Luke. He clasped her gratefully, picked her up and made for the exit. On the way, he noticed, out of the corner of his eye, that Clifford, who had obviously also partaken, was asleep on some bales. Someone had thoughtfully laid him out in the recovery position.

Fresh air, that's what she needs, thought Luke as he hurried with his burden into the cool of the farmyard.

His burden meantime was either giggling uncontrollably, shouting 'yippee' at top decibels, or trying to kiss him.

Luke tried to get Betty to walk, but her legs were of rubber. She needs a place to sleep it off, he decided, and an open doorway and the sweet smell of hay seemed to promise a suitable habitat.

Lowering his responsibilities on to the hay proved more difficult than he might have imagined. He hadn't bargained for the clinging qualities of the inebriated female. Going beyond the point of balance with his load still grimly attached, he found himself in the hay with Betty, and she was kissing him with an expertise which took him by surprise.

"Stop this, enough, just stop," his better nature struggled with difficulty to the surface. "It's not right, not like this, you're . . . well, you're drunk as a Lord."

"Don't you mean a Lady?" she giggled uncontrollably. "Your Ma' said I was to enjoy myself, let my hair down; don't you ever listen to your Ma' Luke?" With surprising strength she pulled him down again.

Luke could resist no longer; he was a man lost in the snow who finally succumbs to sleep; he had been high principled for several minutes now, he had tried . . . he moved in for the kill.

A piercing scream shook the rafters. Luke drew back abruptly. He had never had a reaction like that before.

Betty was sitting up, her eyes large and frightened. "Over there," she pointed. "It moved, it squeaked, it was horrible." She screamed again and pointed. "Little beady eyes, over there."

Luke followed her pointing finger. A tell-tale movement in the hay followed by squeaks told him that their companions were rats. "Just rats," he said. "Probably mating."

Betty got up. Standing on shaky legs she said. "I feel awful, take me home Luke."

Making her as comfortable as possible in the van, Luke turned his thoughts to Clifford. "You'll be all right . . ." but Betty was already fast asleep in that untidy inelegant way that goes with over indulgence. He looked at her, dishevelled now, and in some disarray. His eyes softened, and kissing her softly on the forehead he went in search of his other client.

Spotting Blackie near the door, Luke, unwilling to face a lot of questions, delegated the job of collecting Clifford.

"How's the liddle ole maid?" Blackie wanted to know. "Rare liddle ole dancer sure 'nuff."

"She's none the worse . . . I hope," said Luke.

"You be a lucky chap, could do worse," opined Blackie.

Luke sighed. "She's not my girl."

Blackie grinned. "Reck'n she ha' drawn a bead on ee lad, she'll get ee in the end. Right, I war just about to leave anyway, I'll get that ole lad fur ee."

Blackie collected the supine Clifford, retrieved the pitcher and went round the barn taking leave of his friends, Clifford meantime, draped like an unwanted raincoat over his shoulder.

At the other end of the car ride, Luke hoped that he managed to carry the bodies to their respective beds with a degree of stealth. Any stray sounds of intemperance, he was sure would in any case be laid at his door.

* * *

The car was at the door. The suitcases in the kitchen, Clifford was outside discussing with Martha and Mogford the prospect of coming for a short break, perhaps in the spring; on his own this time. There was so much of interest to him around the farm. The dung hill for instance; full of life.

Luke waited in the kitchen for Betty. She came down, looking better for a night's sleep. Her eyelids were lowered and her glasses swung from one hand.

Luke took the glasses from her hand and fitted them gently, with all the care of an optician suiting a client. "I like you just as much with them on," he said gently.

She looked at him then and he saw the love in her eyes.

He took her gently in his arms where she fluttered for a moment like a captive bird, then lay still and secure against him. On tiptoe she could just reach his ear. "I'm in love with you," she whispered, and then she was gone.

Luke watched until the car was lost to sight. He could only stare in wonderment. Betty Pringle really loved him. She had said so. As the car disappeared he was aware of a sense of loss.

Back in the kitchen Mogford said to Martha. "That boy looks as if he has just fallen in love."

Martha looked through the window at Luke, still gazing up the lane, Betty's words echoing over and over in his brain. "You're right Mogford, I'd recognise that look anywhere." She smiled. Luke had made his mother very happy.

* * *

Although another spring was just round the corner, Martha's spirits were at a low ebb. This year the small wild daffodils would bloom over Hammy's last resting place.

Martha looked at the rug by the Aga, seeming large now without Hammy's spread out bulk. She sighed. Things seemed to happen to them around Christmas, and this was something even Mogford couldn't put right.

They had all been so happy after the visit from Betty and Clifford. Luke had been on cloud nine. He had seen Betty since. Tickets had arrived for the theatre from Luke's stunning, shimmering, silver songstress, now established in the lead role, and Luke had gone backstage with Betty on his arm.

Martha let her thoughts drift around Luke. She recognised that a new maturity sat comfortably on him. He was involved in the new expanded Mogford dealership, handling routine contracts, transport arrangements, maintaining contact with the 'up country' dealers, and leaving Mogford free to pursue his opportunist local dealing. Yes he had finally grown up, and it seemed as if he and Betty would make a go of it.

There would be wedding bells, Martha felt sure. A sigh escaped her. It was what she wanted; of course it was, but she had to face the fact that Luke no longer needed her. No more escapades; no more scrapes to rescue him from; she supposed all mothers had to navigate these difficult waters; but no amount of rationalising made her feel any better.

* * *

It had happened two weeks before Christmas. Martha came down as usual and set about her chores. It was some minutes before she realised that there had been no greeting from Hammy. Even at his laziest he would flick his tail or raise his head. There was nothing. Martha looked at him, in his usual position, apparently fast asleep. It was then that shock and horror hit her with a stunning blow. Hammy was a noisy sleeper. Groans and snuffles and twitches, and now he was still, and peaceful, without movement. Hammy was dead.

Martha fell into a chair, the blood drained from her face. Shaken and close to fainting she was incapable of movement; and there Mogford found her.

Mogford came into the kitchen dragging his trouser braces over his shoulders and smiling cheerfully. He caught sight of Martha, and followed her eyes fixed unblinkingly on Hammy, and he was kneeling by her patting her hands. "I'll get you some hot sweet tea m'dear, you're in shock," he said. Mogford bustled about making tea. He called up the stairs. "Bring a blanket Luke, your mother's not well."

Luke rushed down and wrapped his mother in a blanket warm from his own bed. They shared tears, the three of them, and Luke shrouded Hammy in a sheet and buried him deep in the daffodil field.

Martha had been living with her grief and mood of black despair for the best part of four months when Hamish McKay phoned and asked her to tea. Martha agreed in lacklustre fashion. Once this would have been an occasion to savour, now she agreed mechanically to the arrangements, and duly met Hamish in the tea-room where they had previously celebrated Martha's one and only entry into Mogford's dealing affairs.

Hamish was concerned by Martha's changed appearance. "You've lost weight lass," he said, but he was even more disturbed by her lack of animation. She had lost that vital spark, the zest for life. It was as if the world had become a dreary place for Martha, and it showed on her face.

"We'll have tea, then you will talk," said Hamish firmly. "You will talk until you have told me every little detail of every little problem that's troubling you. I don't suppose you have told Mogford the half of it. We will sit here till you have talked your fill; even if they start putting the chairs on the tables."

They had tea, exchanging desultory conversation, but Martha had little appetite.

Soon Hamish was pushing his chair back. He crossed his legs and folded his arms. "Now," he said. "I'm listening."

"There's really not much to tell," began Martha. "Hammy died, it was a shock . . ."

An hour later a waitress asked if they would like another pot of tea, and Hamish nodded.

"Goodness I have been going on. How long have I been talking?"

"Only about an hour. Confession's good for the soul."

Another pot of tea arrived, and Martha realised she felt a little better. Hamish was easy to talk to, just the odd question, a comment here and there. She could feel his concern and his warmth. But how on earth could she have talked so long, there was little enough to tell.

Indeed as Hamish told Mogford on the phone that night, there was nothing wrong with Martha that time wouldn't heal. She was missing Hammy more than anyone could guess, and she had to get used to the fact that her mother role was coming to an end. He had another suggestion which Mogford discussed later with Martha.

"It's like this m'dear," he said. "Luke has a lot on his plate, what with doing the Fortescue horses, that little factory out there, and all the extra dealership work. He needs a bit of help."

"We could give up the hessian gloves," said Martha doubtfully, and I suppose Luke doesn't need to do the horses. That is, not where the money's concerned."

"True," agreed Mogford. "But that production line is something we do together, and Luke has endless fun refining the machinery all the time. Then there's the horses. Luke has a fondness for those animals now, and of course he gets some riding without us keeping a horse."

"He's quite thick with Percy now as well," agreed Martha. "We might see him riding point to point one day."

"Too much solid bone and muscle for that," laughed

Mogford. "But . . . getting back to Hamish . . . he suggests we have a live-in boy."

"You mean, live in, with us, as family?"

"Yes, Hamish is in touch with some organisation. It would be a lad from a deprived background. A poor lad, town bred, we'd be giving him a chance. That is, of course, if you feel you could cope. He might have a few problems m'dear."

"I expect I could manage, not all my pupils were born with silver spoons. I managed then, I expect I could manage now."

Mogford smiled. Martha had spoken tartly. It was the first sign of spirit that had broken through her apathy.

Three weeks later the boy arrived. He was just sixteen years old and his name was Tony Goodwin. He had benefited from some corrective training in an institution, and was totally innocent of any knowledge of country life. He had a wide grin and a devil may care look about him. Martha took to him from the word go.

The next market day, Mogford arrived home as usual but did not come inside immediately. Martha, Luke, and Tony were at the table enjoying a cup of tea. They looked towards the door expectantly. Why the delay? Mogford usually breezed in . . . but the door was being pushed open slowly; still no Mogford.

Martha lowered her angle of vision and saw it. "Oh my God, it's Hammy, come back as a puppy."

Three pairs of eyes watched fascinated, as the puppy plodding on unsteady legs, stepped on a trailing ear, freed itself, plodded on, and collapsed on the rug by the Aga. It flicked a tail tip and looked up with red rimmed eyes to behold his new family.

At this point Mogford bounced in, beaming. "What do you think m'dear?" he asked.

But Martha and Tony were on their knees on the rug. The new member was rolling over to have his tummy rubbed.

Luke caught his father's eye. "I think she likes it Da'. But how did you get it? The markings, almost identical to poor old Hammy."

"The dealer network," replied Mogford. "I circulated photos. Dealers from Cornwall to the North Midlands have been on the look-out. It's Hammy the second all right."

Martha looked up and her eyes were shining. "We'll call him Hammy Second," she said.

Mogford smiled at her. With a deprived boy to care for and a pup to housetrain, he felt that Martha would soon be on the road to recovery.

13

A pony for Clare

"I think it's a shame. The poor mite has only just about learned to walk, let alone sit on a horse," said Martha indignantly.

"Well," argued Luke reasonably. "Her legs are just about long enough to go either side of a saddle, and her dad should know best."

It was breakfast time, and Luke had mentioned that Percy Percival was looking for a suitable pony for his little Clare.

Martha returned to the attack. "She might fall off and hurt herself, and besides she has no say in the matter, she's too young to make up her mind, and it *is* unfair, and just another example of a dominant father."

"I would hardly call Percy dominant, quite the opposite, and as I understand it Belinda is all in favour." Mogford contributed his view mildly.

"So you're against me as well Mogford. That leaves Tony. Who do you side with Tony?"

Tony busily addressing his bacon and eggs, and not too sure what it was all about, said, with the diplomacy learned in institutions, foster homes and from the sum total of his early life, "I agree with *you* Mrs Mogford." Food and comfort were important to Tony, and Martha represented both.

Mogford frowned at Tony across the table. "You were late up this morning, and late in last night."

"All work and no play," said Luke. "The lad's got to have *some* fun."

"You would know about that," said Martha. "Now leave Tony be, we were talking about this pony. I don't suppose anything I say will change anything."

"I'm afraid not m'dear. Percy was practically brought up on a horse. Belinda much the same. Even our Luke is a considerable horseman now. Not much we ordinary mortals can do."

Martha snorted. "No use trying to get round me now Mogford. I'm disappointed in you." She got up and bustled about clearing the table. "I expect you men can find some work to do."

"I've only one suggestion," said Mogford. "The pony should be small, a Shetland maybe."

"Or an Exmoor perhaps," said Luke. "The October gathering will be soon, then the sale." Luke warmed to his subject. "Let's say Percy bought a young pony, a yearling, or even a mare and foal, Clare could grow up with the pony. By the time it was old enough, and broken in, her legs would be a bit longer."

Pleased with his master stroke, he helped himself to another slice of toast, a lead followed quickly by the opportunist Tony.

Martha turned from the sink. "At least you are showing more common sense than your father this morning."

Mogford sighed. He wasn't too sure whether he had incurred Martha's displeasure by not supporting her on the 'Clare's pony' issue, or for his criticism of young Tony. He rather suspected the latter.

Tony had settled in well. Mogford would be the first to admit it. A streetwise boy, he was rapidly becoming countrywise. Sharp witted, quick on the uptake, he was a great help to Luke, and in Martha's eyes he could do no wrong.

If only he was a bit sharper in the mornings. Mogford

got very impatient with people who couldn't get up in the morning. He had suffered from Luke in his earlier days; now it looked as if history was repeating itself. He would have to straighten the lad out. But there was Martha, so protective, a mother hen. Well perhaps he could contain his irritation a little longer.

The morning routine was invariable. Alarms were set for six. All, except on occasion, Tony, would respond. Martha would stoke up the Aga, encourage Hammy Second to toddle outside, wash up any leftovers from the night before, lay up for breakfast, and sally forth to milk Daisy. Luke was on calves and poultry. Mogford worked his way round the various pig houses, feeding and checking. Tony was supposed to follow Mogford's route, mucking out.

Recently, and usually after late nights, Tony would oversleep. These were the mornings which ruffled the Mogford feathers.

* * *

Parked on high ground, Percy's Land Rover provided a useful viewing platform from which to observe the annual gathering of an Exmoor pony herd.

Percy and Luke watched with interest. "Looks like a bit of fun," observed Percy. "Perhaps next year you could get us invited."

Luke laughed. "I might at that, although you're the expert, I'm just a beginner. Anyway some of these ponies could be on sale at the horse fair; that's held on the last Thursday of this month. Just the place to get Clare a steady little pony."

Percy was viewing the scene through binoculars. "Nothing very steady about those little chaps. They're really stretching themselves."

The weather was ideal. A bright October day, the visibility was good, with an autumn chill to cool the frantically racing ponies.

Luke borrowed the glasses. Indeed it was a spectacle. Farmers on a variety of mounts, galloped hither and thither seeking out small groups of ponies herding them together.

Helpers on foot were holding the main body, a mix of mares and foals, with the odd stallion; about thirty or forty milling, steaming, excited, ponies.

"And that's only the half of it," grinned Percy. "They still have to drive them to the farm, sort them out by brand, wean foals; a general once a year sort out. Other herds will be gathered over the next week or so, and any mixed brands sorted out."

"Quite an operation, all over the moor," mused Luke. "I suppose what goes for sale are the ponies not needed for breeding; colt foals, older mares, perhaps the odd stallion that's outlived its usefulness, poorer sorts, that sort of thing."

"True," said Percy, "but there will be others. Ones that have been ridden. Children out here have ponies to ride, and of course they are strong enough to carry an adult. Besides there will be all sorts there apart from Exmoors; I must say I am rather taken with them though."

"Might be too lively for Clare for starters. I started with a real old armchair; that piebald up at the Hall."

Percy smiled. "You were something of a late convert, old boy. Not quite the same thing."

"Well I know what my mother would like for Clare."

"One that's made of wood and runs on four wheels," said Percy drily. "I know what fills my eye. One of these mealy nosed chaps, about five years old, which has been ridden. They are really hardy, could winter out, could be trained up for driving classes at the shows."

"Speaking as a friend," said Luke, "You're getting into areas of expense, spanking round showrings with a rug over your knees, can you afford it?"

"Of course not," Percy grinned. "But if the right pony presents itself, I might be tempted."

"Let's be at the fair anyway. You might end up with an old piebald off a gipsy."

* * *

It was a perfect Exmoor pony, twelve hands high, shaggy coated, with the distinctive meal coloured muzzle, a hallmark of the breed. The auctioneer knew a good pony when he saw one.

"You'll not see anything more typical of the breed today he announced. "Off the high moor, hardy as they come, and well bred. Pure Exmoor, four years old, a child's pony, quiet and warranted sound in every way. Should make a good price, who'll start me. Just trot her up and down, a bit lively like."

The pony was being paraded by a gangling boy who was finding it hard to face up to the parting. If he had hoped there would be no bids he was to be disappointed. The bids came thick and fast.

"A grand little mare, make a good breeder, against you over there sir, come again?" The auctioneer raised an eyebrow at a tall, black eyed man wearing a bright neckerchief.

The man nodded curtly, and directed a threatening stare at Percy, whose bid he had to cap.

"Doesn't look over friendly," observed Percy.

"A gipsy," grinned Luke. "He'll probably cut your throat later. Perhaps you'd better let him have it; he probably has a breeder in mind, 'up country', and you're whittling away at his profit margin."

"If he wants it, he'll have to pay for it," said Percy grimly. "I know a good type when I see it. Besides *I* could breed from it."

The bidding jumped again. Percy and the gipsy now the only contenders.

"Let's go," urged Luke. "You're way over the top now, and besides you came to buy a pony for Clare, not a perfect breed specimen . . . and look over there."

The tall man had been joined by others, equally tall, and dark, and black eyed.

Percy was being subjected to the combined projected malice of two who could have been brothers, and a youth who was a younger version of the original bidder.

Percy surveyed the battery of black eyes. The message was unmistakable. Stop or else . . . Indeed one produced a long slim knife and slowly and deliberately decapitated a brown twist of tobacco.

"Can't stop now old boy. Too much like showing the white feather," Percy whispered.

"Well, if you can't do it for yourself, do it for me," suggested Luke equably. "The odds are not in our favour."

"Two more bids, then I'm out."

"You'll only make them two bids angrier."

The auctioneer was addressing himself to Percy. "Have you finished? Pity to lose this little mare for a few pounds. Thank you Sir," and he was away into his spiel and addressing himself to the group across the way.

Percy's latest bid had thrown the gipsies into a state of agitation. They had obviously left profit behind and now pride was at stake.

Percy threw them a look. Defiant, and with perhaps a tinge of haughtiness. He watched as they talked together, gesticulating, then a bid. They were becoming distinctly disturbed.

Percy's final bid was capped by the gipsies and Luke grabbed Percy's arm. "Time to leave," he said, and hurried Percy from the battleground. "We will mix with the crowd and become as anonymous as possible. We might meet up with my Da', he's here somewhere. If we could recruit a few friends . . . meantime, camouflage is our best bet. Blend into the background. Do try to look less aristocratic Percy, it brings out the worst in some people."

There was no denying the success of Luke's tactics, but Percy soon became impatient.

"Look here," he said. "I came here to buy a pony for Clare, and that's what I'm jolly well going to do, gipsies or no gipsies. You don't have to come if you don't want to."

"All right Percy I'm with you. We'll go and take a look at what's not been in the ring yet. I expect the gipsies are still buying."

Away from the noise and bustle of the sale, the clatter of hooves, the 'hups' and 'giddups' of the vendors, the rise and fall of the auctioneer's delivery, Percy and Luke strolled past the pens of foals and unbroken moor ponies, to where tethered ponies, were quietly munching hay, or being tidied up by their handlers.

"All seems very peaceful," remarked Percy. "Let's see what's about."

"I thought maybe a mare with a foal at foot, would fit the bill," offered Luke.

"What a splendid idea. Clare could ride the mare and the foal would eventually replace her. Good thinking Luke."

"Not quite how I had figured it. I was thinking of selling the mare when the foal was old enough, and by the time Clare was old enough, the foal would be big enough."

"Good heavens Luke. Clare would be about five or even six by then. I don't know any Percival who started that late."

Luke sighed. The Percivals were a breed apart. He had tried. He would explain this to his mother . . .

There was no time for further conjecture. Their progress was barred by four figures who had materialised magically. Luke guessed they had been crouching behind tethered ponies; and there was no escape. He and Percy stood rooted, and awaited developments.

The bidder, it appeared, was to be the spokesman. He stood directly in front of his captives, while the others deployed in a circle, to cover any attempt at escape.

The man spoke. "We be peaceable folk, us gipsies. That is if no one annoys us. But us is annoyed wi' ee maister." He pierced Percy with his black eyes. "Us reck'ns ee owes us a bit o' luck on that there liddle ol' pony."

"See the vendor," said Percy stoutly. "He's the one who owes a 'luck penny'."

"Not how us sees it," replied the gipsy. "Ee did cost us profit, an' more, on the biddin'. Us'll settle for, break even." He mentioned a figure.

Out of the corner of his eye Percy noticed that one of the gipsies had again produced a knife and was paring tobacco. "I beg leave to consult with my friend. Perhaps you and your accomplices would be good enough to step back a yard or two."

"Us'll grant ee that," said the spokesman. "Just step back a couple o' paces lads."

"What have you to offer then, Percy; martial arts, kung fu, karate . . . a sword stick perhaps?"

"I boxed at university, I had a very good straight left. I won several cups as a bantam weight."

Luke groaned. "These chaps don't know anything about the Queensberry rules. What weight are you now?"

"Probably featherweight, what about you?"

"A few fights behind pubs . . . when I was younger, of course. Came off second best quite often. I take it you haven't thought of just paying up?"

A look of astonishment appeared on Percy's face.

"All right, all right," said Luke. "A Percival doesn't . . . in the meantime get out your wallet, pretend to be counting. It'll buy us a little time while we wait for a miracle to happen."

The gipsies waited stoically as their victims produced wallets, counted and argued, while fifty yards away a miracle was hurrying towards them on twinkling legs.

Mogford arrived a little breathless. Earlier he had found Ben Loverage in the crowd and had enlisted his aid in the matter of an elderly piebald mare with foal at foot. They had viewed the ambush from afar, and Mogford had hurried on leaving Ben to stand by in case of dire need.

Entering the circle, he beamed all round. "A gathering of friends?" he enquired.

"Not exactly," said the spokesman. "This 'ere young gent is just 'bout to 'and over some money."

Mogford could see from the proud tilt of Percy's head that this was far from the case. He held up his hand as Percy was about to disclaim.

"Me first Percy," he said sternly. "I have some business with these gents." He turned to the gipsy spokesman. "If you would step aside with me, we could talk privately."

Out of earshot he said, "Before we discuss my business, tell me what trouble you have with these two young men."

"Well maister," said the gipsy, "we be fair aggravated by these two, especially the young toff. It be like this . . ." The gipsy talked and Mogford listened, nodding, and asking the odd question.

The gipsy's recital of his grievance came to an end and he asked Mogford, "Now what business were ee thinkin' o' havin' wi' me?"

"I was looking at a mare with foal at foot. My old friend Ben Loverage tells me it's yours. He says you don't want to part with the old lady, so I'm prepared to offer over market price." He named a figure. "That's my best offer take it or leave it, and if you take it, you shake hands with those two young men over there." He turned and with his fingers in his mouth he let loose a piercing whistle.

A head popped up, grinning cheerfully over the withers of a tethered horse.

"Over here Ben, I want you to meet some friends," he called.

Mogford turned again to the gipsy. "Do we have a deal?"

The gipsy nodded, notes were exchanged, and hands were clapped all round.

Ben arrived and greeted Luke like a blood brother.

"Friends of yours?" grunted the gipsy.

"Took us in, me an' my liddle ole donkey, when the snow was deep an' the wind blew cold."

"Fair enough. We be cousins I reck'n. You've been away?"

Ben nodded. "I'm the black sheep."

The other man spoke again. "That liddle ole 'chavvie' over there is gettin' wed. Reck'n us'll see ee at the weddin'." He gave Ben a time and a place and turned away abruptly. Catching Mogford's eye, the semblance of a smile crossed his face.

"Reck'n you did your sums just 'bout right maister," he said. "A pleasure doin' business wi' ee."

When the gipsies had gone, a beaming Mogford said, "Come and see my purchases."

The mare was small and tired and old, but she had a lively colt foal beside her.

"The old girl needs a good home, but she'll be fine as a starter pony for Clare, and the colt will follow on in time."

"You mean . . ." Percy was taken aback. "You bought them for Clare?"

"Well not exactly. I thought if I sold the pair to you, say, for a pound, that would make me the vendor. Then I would be entitled to a 'bit of luck'."

"And how much would that cost me?" asked Percy.

"Just what you would have parted with to the gipsies, one way or another, less the pound. That way I will be giving Clare a present at proper market value."

"And you and I haven't lost any teeth, or suffered any pain. I think you are getting a good deal," said Luke.

Percy was looking at Mogford open mouthed. "In effect you bought those gipsies off. Now you're recharging me. It was a face saving exercise on my account."

"Well," said Mogford reasonably. "I didn't want to see those patrician features rearranged, or Luke come to any harm. You could say it was face saving."

"And you are giving me an old mare, to make sure Clare has a safe first mount," grinned Percy. "Martha will be pleased."

"Deal?" said Mogford.

"Deal," said Percy, slapping hands. "As I always say," he went on, "if you are going to be manipulated, it's best done by friends."

Later, as Mogford recounted the events of the day to Martha, he pointed out not only the steadiness of the old mare, but the benefits of a good home and a light rider to the pony. Summing up the brush with the gipsies he said. "You know m'dear, everything has a cost. Take pride for instance, the sort that's in the breeding, like Percy's death before dishonour, that sort of thing. It has to be paid for. I think I was right to pass on the cost, don't you m'dear?"

"Pride goes before a fall," quoted Martha.

"As you say," said Mogford. "Then there's that other one. He who pays the piper, calls the tune."

14
Armageddon

EARTH moving equipment was massed a mile and a half from the village. There was no doubt now about the route. A wide swath would soon be cut across the cricket field. The road from town had been widened, now the village by-pass was the logical next step.

So far, the vicar had not felt obliged to offer himself before the bulldozers. Perhaps he was saving himself till the hallowed sod of the pitch should be violated.

Mogford and his committee had fought tooth and nail for a roundabout where the new road would divert from the original. This battle had been won. Tourists would be able to leave the main road easily and follow the signs to 'B & B', 'pub', 'shop' and any other points of financial gain to the villagers.

One section of the populace was completely happy, the cricketers were less so. The vicar was still bemoaning the loss of a village amenity, and the fact of his being deprived, in his twilight years of playing against the 'County'.

Mogford, Percy and Bob, had applied themselves to the problem, and Mogford was given a free hand to pursue one of his ideas.

There was a long way to go, but Mogford hoped he might yet save the vicar from a dramatic confrontation with the earth movers.

* * *

The bulldozer blade had encroached three feet into the outfield, only six inches from the prone figure of the vicar. He lay as it were, to attention. The scuffed toes of his shoes pointed heavenwards, as did the sharp point of his thin nose; his arms stiffly by his sides, the thumbs following a give and take line along the wrinkled seams of his trousers. His eyelids were lowered; there was an air of rumpled dignity about him as he prepared to martyr himself for the cause.

High above him the driver surveyed the rapidly gathering crowd from his vantage point. He scratched his head. "Come on some o' you lads," he appealed. "You all know me, us plays in the team together, I lives in the village, drag that there ol' scarecrow out o' my road." There was no response to this disrespectful suggestion, and the reverend showed not a flicker.

"How long 'as ee been like this, mate?" asked Blackie who had just arrived on the scene. It looked as though he was prepared for a long wait as a small pitcher swung from a finger.

" 'Bout an hour, I got here for eight, hardly got the machine started 'afore he were streakin' out o' the vicarage as if the devil were on 'is tail. Language were a bit choice too. For a vicar, that is. He's been quiet since he laid down; he a'n't dead is ee?"

Blackie inspected. "His chest do move a bit, reck'n he be livin'. Want a drop of refreshment vicar?" He proffered the pitcher, but there was no response. Blackie perched on the bulldozer blade, expertly flicked the vessel over his wrist, raised it and had a long drink. "Might as well sit a while," he observed. " 'Tis a nice enough day."

"That it is Blackie," Bob approached on his blind side. He waved away the cider. "I might as well rest a bit, not as young as I once was." He tied his little dog to a convenient part of the bulldozer and seated himself alongside Blackie. A few others began to seat themselves on or around the machine.

"We'll soon have a committee quorum," said Bob as Percy appeared leading his piebald pony mare with little Clare on board.

Percy tied the pony to the bulldozer and lifted Clare down. "Maybe Clare could take Freddie for a little walk Bob," he suggested, as Blackie made room on the blade.

"Fine," said Bob. "All we need now is for Mogford to appear and we could have a committee meeting."

The next arrival was dressed in blue and pushed a bicycle.

"Mornin' Will, come an' 'ave a drop o' good stuff," Blackie was getting a glow on.

"No thank ee Blackie, not on duty, now what's all this, it do look like an unlawful gathering, I 'as to ask ee all to disperse." At this point he noticed the prone body of the vicar now almost totally obscured by sitters. "My god, we need an ambulance, he a'n't dead be ee?"

Having reassured himself that the vicar was indeed breathing, and not wishing to incur his ecclesiastical wrath by forcing the issue, he spent the next quarter of an hour, coaxing, cajoling, and threatening a totally unimpressed gathering. Finally with an exasperated, "Shit, I might as well join you," he sat down.

High in his eyrie, the driver was suffering from boredom. There was no officialdom in sight. He descended and squeezed into a space on one of the 'dozer arms. "Reck'n I can sit on my own machine," he grumbled. "Pass me that there liddle ole pitcher, Blackie."

Luke heard about the gathering while on an errand to the village shop. By the time he reached the group a party atmosphere prevailed. The pitcher had been replaced by a keg which sat, broached, and available to all, on one of the bulldozer's tracks. Mrs May had arrived with a basket of sandwiches and advice on how to deal with the vicar, whom she had not quite forgiven. With the sandwiches she was handing out remarks like, 'I can always rush back and fetch a spade,' or, 'where's the grave digger? He's never around when there's a bit o' work to do.'

Luke surveyed the scene. An elderly pony tethered, droop lipped, head hanging; a child and a little dog playing; a motley group, quaffing, eating and exchanging garbled conversation. Through a forest of dangling legs and nodding heads, he spotted the vicar, prone and silent, but now wrapped in blankets, supplied by those who knew about such things as shock and hypothermia. Only his nose and shabby shoes protruded from this tight roll. "He isn't . . .?" asked Luke.

"No, no," replied Blackie. "He be more comfortable there than he be in that great ole vicarage. He be an expert on that there yoga stuff. Not very Christian if ee asks me."

"Yoga! I doubt it," said Luke.

"Oh, I don' know, us 'as been talking 'bout it. Ee do get up to some funny things since his missus passed on."

Luke reflected on this. True the vicar had become more eccentric, more shabby and more skeletal with each passing year since the loss of his partner, and there had been odd happenings. There was that time when he had been spotted in the early hours striding up and down the cricket pitch dressed only in a night shirt, and it was true his temper was controlled by a very short fuse. But yoga, he hadn't heard of that one. Luke smiled to himself, and looked again at the motley gathering. A suggestion by someone would become a fact in an hour. Still the vicar had maintained his immobile state for a very long time.

"I think I'm going to fetch my Da'." Luke addressed himself to Bob and Percy, who had resisted Blackie's hospitality. "Then you chaps can have a committee meeting."

The committee meeting was duly held, a little apart and viewed with interest by a group of Mogford's sheep. Mogford noted with satisfaction that they all looked in lamb. Martha had drawn his attention to crocuses in the garden. Before they knew it lambing would be upon them. He turned his attention to the business in hand.

After the meeting Blackie was called over. "We want you to explain something to your mates," said Mogford. "Keep it short, if you can, and make it clear that we have a plan well advanced and the digging can go ahead. Not today though by the state of the driver. You'd better carry him home afterwards. Get all the people away and leave the vicar to me."

Mogford inspected his sheep till everyone had gone. He approached the vicar, still prone and looking very peaceful.

Luke had passed on the popular view that the vicar was on a par with mystics of the Far East as far as yoga was concerned. Mogford had always been amazed at the effect of Blackie's cider on perfectly normal people. He shook the vicar gently and unwound his wrappings. The response was a fierce snort, followed by a shake of the head, then the eyes opened and the vicar sat up and yawned. "Where am I?" he asked drowsily.

Mogford grinned. "You are six inches away from a bulldozer blade. Here let me help you up."

On his feet the vicar yawned again and stretched luxuriously. "That's the best sleep I've had in weeks," he said. "You know, perhaps, that I am a chronic insomniac?"

Mogford nodded. "I've heard of you walking the cricket pitch at night."

"It was after they put those blankets round me; so kind and the sound of people enjoying themselves; I was so comfortable and warm, and there was a bit of sun on my face; I just drifted off." He smiled sheepishly. "I feel a bit guilty, indeed," he said. "Not much of a protest, enjoying a nap in the sun."

"In fact, it was very effective, everybody put it down to

mind over matter. Anyway it'll be our secret, between the three of us."

"Three?" queried the vicar.

"Him up there," said Mogford.

"Oh, Him, yes of course," said the vicar.

15
The factory

"I don't like it, not one little bit. You'll have to take Luke in hand," said Martha.

"It's not that easy," worried Mogford. "I don't like it any more than you do, but Luke's a grown man, might even soon be a married man, if all those trips up to London are anything to go by. I can't just tell him not to get involved. He knows my views on the subject."

"I think it's the machinery that's the attraction. He always was fascinated by machines, and particularly designing and building them. Look at that production line out there, how he's worked on it and refined it."

"Oh, he's got the talent for machinery all right. We just have to hope he doesn't get carried away, get involved financially, that's my worry."

Mogford had stayed on after breakfast to discuss his latest worry with Martha. Luke had become increasingly involved in helping a friend to refurbish a recently acquired factory in town. The end product was to be package mouldings in expanded polystyrene. Finance was of the shoestring variety, and Mogford's fear was that Luke would, willy nilly, be drawn into taking a share of the business.

Never one to waste time, Martha was washing up as they talked. She thumped some soapy crockery on the draining board.

"This polystyrene, is it here to stay?" she demanded.

"Oh yes," said Mogford. "It's been around for a few years already. It's the packaging material of the future. It is very big business, and that's where my worry lies. A good new product and a wide open market has attracted big business people with capital and expertise. That factory in town is out of date already. I don't see Luke's friend surviving."

"I expect the last owners saw him coming," said Martha. "Seems like his best bet is to cut his losses. But he won't of course. These young men are always ready to rush in where angels fear to tread. Well, you have to do something about it, Mogford. Now be off with you, you have already spoilt my day."

"Well m'dear," he said heavily. "I don't seem to have done much up to now. Talking to Luke has just, I think, made him more determined to stick by his friend, and now I've put you into a bad mood."

Martha turned from the sink. Wiping soapy arms on a towel, she said, "It's not you Mogford, you will sort it out in your own time, I know. Meantime if you want to put me in a good mood, you can buy me a new dress for the Farmers' Ball. It's this week you know."

"And you haven't a thing to wear. Right, this is something I *can* sort out. Get your hat and coat, we're going shopping. At least," he added reflectively, "I haven't the problem of what to wear. My dinner suit is as good as new."

* * *

"I can't think why you don't get yourself a full set of tails. That dinner suit fits where it touches," observed Martha.

"Which is everywhere. It's too tight, you have to face it Da', you've put on weight," said Luke helpfully.

Mogford squirmed under their combined scrutiny. "It fitted me when I bought it."

"That was twenty years ago," said Martha severely. "There will be lots there tonight in white tie and tails."

"Some of your dealer friends should have horns as well," said Luke. "But honestly Da', that top trouser button is ready to pop. Tell you what, wear a cummerbund, it'll give you a more dashing look anyway, and undo the top button. Otherwise you hardly have room for a half pint, let alone a big dinner."

"I don't expect your Da' will drink much," said Martha pointedly. "But I agree a cummerbund would look smart."

"And he's got the waist for it," suggested Luke.

Mogford sighed. "I enjoy the 'Farmers' Ball' once a year, it's the getting ready that plagues me. All right, find that waistband you were talking about, and m'dear if you would check if my tie is straight."

Martha straightened his bow, and took a clothes brush to his jacket. "Just go easy on the drink tonight Mogford," she warned. "I know what you're like when you get among your cronies, and they'll all be there tonight."

"Well m'dear, I have to be sociable," protested Mogford.

"You *want* to be sociable more like. I know you Mogford, you like to enjoy yourself. And no impromptu cabaret. Last year it was singing barbers, but the year before . . ."

"Yes, yes, that was a bit over the top, so I was told, but no, m'dear, this time you can depend on it. I won't even take my tie off."

"You look really nice in your new dress Mrs Mogford," Tony who had been sharing the comforts of the Aga with Hammy Second, chipped in his ha'pennyworth.

He was rewarded with a warm look from Martha. "Thank you Tony. At least someone noticed. Come Mogford let's be off."

"Don't worry Da'. We'll cover for you in the morning if you are a bit . . . you know . . . tired."

Mogford bristled. "When did I ever . . ."

"This time last year, and the year before. Especially the year before."

Martha was at the door. "Mogford."

He was by her side in an instant. "Yes m'dear, we're wasting good socialising time."

It was only once a year; he fully intended to have a good time; all his best friends would be there; of course he had no intention of over indulging.

But as Martha might on occasion be heard to quote, 'The road to hell is paved with good intentions.'

It was six in the morning. Alarm clocks were whirring and jangling in different bedrooms. Martha reached out to still the clangour at the bedside and turned to look at Mogford. She smiled. There was no way he was going to make it to the pig house this morning.

She was still smiling as she set about her morning chores. It had been a good evening. She had enjoyed it. Mogford had behaved very well . . . up to a point.

It was perhaps a little unfortunate that he had climbed on to the stage and sung that market song; and some of those jokes were a bit questionable, to say the least; still he had brought the house down; she was rather proud of him. It was after that, what with all the back slapping and people buying him drinks, that he had, well, become rather over indulged.

Martha could hardly blame him for being popular, and was inclined to take a rather charitable view of the whole thing. She would let him sleep.

Out in the stock buildings, Tony was manfully trying to cope with the Mogford load as well as his own. Of late, having moderated his late nights Tony's performance in the morning was exemplary.

"You're doing a good job," observed Luke, passing through. "However, I think you ought to give the boss a call. He won't be over pleased if he finds you have done all his work. You know what he's like about sleeping in."

"Are you sure Luke, he won't be angry with me?" Tony had no wish to blot a fairly clean copybook.

"Take my word for it," said Luke seriously. "Make sure

he gets up." He went off whistling loudly, leaving Tony with his dilemma.

Well if Luke said so . . . he supposed . . . He headed for the farmhouse. He kicked off his boots and entered. Martha was by this time in the cowshed, milking Daisy. Hammy Second raised a sleepy head.

"Mr Mogford, Mr Mogford, time to get up," called Tony tentatively. There was no reply so Tony increased the volume. "Mr Mogford, time to get up," he called sharply. For a moment there was no response, then, "Just coming, I'm up and about." Tony smiled. He stole up the stairs in stockinged feet.

Mogford was deeply unconscious. "Just coming, I'm up and about," he slurred.

Tony made it to the kitchen before laughter overtook him.

Later he discussed his little adventure with Martha, and after she had chided Luke for his part in it, and when she had recovered from a fit of the giggles, she put things in perspective for Tony.

"It's a once a year lapse," she explained. "We won't remind Mogford of it, but at least it let you see what you must have looked like when the boot was on the other foot, so to speak."

Martha could not at this point resist a quote from her national bard: 'O wad some Pow'r the giftie gie us, to see oursels as others see us.'

Tony thought he got the drift.

* * *

"Well this is it," said Luke as he stopped the car outside a rather dilapidated wooden building. "What do you think?"

"It's not exactly prepossessing, at least not from the outside," replied Mogford. "And the approaches, past the concrete works, then the rubbish tip, and the road is worse than our farm lane."

"A coat of paint here and there, the odd loose board nailed up," said Luke cheerfully. "Come inside, it's better than the outside and anyway the main purpose of the exercise is to meeting Jim Comer, and Sally his wife. I understand you have decided you know her father."

"That's right. Once you told me what her maiden name was, I made the connection. He's a good friend although we're not on visiting terms; he farms on that red soil down south. I see him around the markets, we have a deal now and then, but I haven't seen Sally since she was a little girl."

"Well, she's a big girl now," grinned Luke, and Mogford had to agree, shaking hands a few minutes later. It was patently obvious that, not only was she pregnant, but that the birth was not far off.

He found Jim to be personable, energetic and with a boundless enthusiasm for the project. Mogford listened to his business philosophy, making mental notes. It was high risk and carried too great an element of personal preference and optimism. It appeared also that Jim found it difficult to work on the family farm with his father, especially with the prospect of another mouth to feed. His father apparently was not over generous and Jim wanted something better for his wife and child.

Mogford didn't like it. There were too many non business factors getting in the way. He summed up. "So what it boils down to, is, make a quick killing with what equipment you have here – you base this on an under supplied market – then retool the factory to face the stiffer competition as the market becomes more competitive."

"That's about it," said Jim. "It's something of a gamble maybe, but it's the only way we can do it."

"Perhaps I could have a look round," suggested Mogford.

"You would do better with Luke as escort, I don't think I could have got this far without his help. He's toolmaker, pipe fitter, you name it, and he also nurses that old boiler in the corner."

Mogford regarded the boiler with mistrust. "It's a bit vintage isn't it?"

"An old coal burner, converted to oil. It supplies steam to expand the beads and cook the mouldings. A bit out of your element aren't you Da'?" Luke had taken his father in hand for the guided tour.

"You're right there son," said Mogford looking apprehensively at the hissing old boiler. "There seems to be steam leaking out of everywhere. Those pipes for instance."

"Don't worry Da', it's not about to blow up, that's new pipework. Steam always tests new joints. It'll seal itself in a few days. Now, this revolving drum is a batch pre-expander where the raw material is changed from a sugar like substance to little beads. These are autoclaves where the mouldings are cooked, venturi guns for filling the moulds; in here the toolroom . . ." There was no doubting Luke's enthusiasm, but it was the keenness of the technician, the challenge of the outdated machines, not the cold calculation of the businessman.

The journey home gave Luke the opportunity to fill in the little items he may have overlooked during the tour. Mogford's head was spinning. Much of the technical detail was a confusion to him. One word kept crossing his mind. It was 'batch'. Batch pre-expanding, batch cooking and cooling. There was no continuous process, no production line, too much manual handling. It was labour intensive and did not flow. He had to research more up to date production methods.

He felt that Jim's optimism was misplaced . . . and there was a baby due any minute. He had some thinking to do. Jim had used up most of his cash to buy the factory. Mogford's only advice on the day had been to protect his asset such as it was, and not to economise on the insurance.

Mogford sighed. He had taken an interest in the first

place, only to keep Luke clear of involvement. Now he couldn't help thinking of that girl, so young, and so pregnant, and that young Jim, so full of hope and belief in himself.

Yes, he had some thinking to do.

* * *

"What's wrong with Daisy?" asked Tony. "She's been mooing since we got up this morning."

"There's only two things that a cow creates about," replied Luke between spoonfuls of porridge. "She either wants a drink of water or she's 'bulling'."

"Luke," Martha was scandalised. "Don't use those coarse expressions in the house, certainly not at breakfast, and not in front of Tony."

"Well Ma," said Luke. "She had an automatic drinking bowl in front of her, so it can't be water. I reckon she's coming into oestrus. What do you think Da'?"

"I think if she is, it's bad news, especially for Daisy. She's been inseminated three times already. I thought she was in calf this time. She'll soon be going dry. How long since her last calf m'dear?"

"Oh several months," said Martha evasively.

"More like seven months," said Mogford. "How much is she giving?"

"Enough, several pints at least," Martha was on the defensive. "I think we should give her one more chance."

"Perhaps you're right m'dear," agreed Mogford. I would hate to sell her as a barrener. We were maybe a bit quick getting rid of the last one."

Luke reached for the phone. "I'll ring the Insemination Centre. The chap must be getting to know his way down here, this will be his fourth visit. I'll arrange for a call tomorrow."

"Meantime, Tony," said Mogford. "You had better let her out. She's making so much noise we can't hear ourselves think, and I want to talk to Luke."

"Right Mr Mogford. Will she find her own way to the field? Is the gate open?"

"Yes Tony, the gate's open. Just turn her loose, she'll make her own way to the field. Now Luke, when you're ready, I want to talk to you." It was six weeks since Mogford had visited the factory. In the meantime he had learned a lot about expanded polystyrene. He knew about injection moulding, continuous flow pre-expanders, and machines that made ceiling tiles.

When he had Luke's full attention he said, "I am more and more convinced that Jim's equipment is too slow and too labour intensive to compete, or even handle big orders quickly enough. In the present climate, it appears everyone wants a supply instantly. Let's say he has ten orders and all want considerable quantities quickly, I can only see him keeping one customer happy. So . . . how far am I off the mark?"

"You've just about summed it up Da'. People are cancelling because he can't produce quickly enough; he's lost several good orders. Also some are not in a hurry to pay and he's running short of the 'ready'. The two big companies who supply the beads, are not so tolerant about credit. In a nutshell he soon will have a cash flow problem. He is going to need a bit of help Da'."

"What he is able to produce is profitable?"

"Oh yes, there's a fair margin in it, although he rather underestimated the waste factor, unmarketable batches and so on; it's not so precise a science as injection moulding."

"And he has wages to pay now, I understand, and is working two shifts. Wages have to be paid whatever." said Mogford.

"That's right Da'. Four men to pay. Jim's right worried, I can tell you, and Sally's getting bigger by the minute."

"Even one customer probably wants these things by the thousand," pondered Mogford. "Let's say he has only one customer. This client builds up his stock and doesn't re-order for a time, or his business gets into trouble, Jim is left with a gap, no good to Jim having his eggs in one basket; and then there's all the big boys better equipped. What he needs is a well filled order book and the capacity to keep everybody happy. I think he'll be hard pushed to hang on, let alone earn enough to re-tool."

"I think you're right Da', and I feel real bad about it. We go back a long way; Young Farmers' Club and all that. I do have some money of my own, perhaps I can help him out a bit."

"You are going to need that, my lad. Being married is an expensive business. I think you and Betty are heading in that direction?"

"You have a way of hitting the nail on the head Da'. Well maybe you can think of something?"

"I'll see what I can do. I'll go and see him again," said Mogford thoughtfully. "Now, have you organised the inseminator?"

"Tomorrow morning."

At breakfast next morning Martha expressed a view. "Sperm in a bottle," she snorted. "I never did hold with it."

"Ma," exclaimed Luke in mock horror. "It's a good job Tony's gone out already, that's all I can say."

16
A finger of suspicion

CONSTABLE Walters was decidedly ill at ease. He stood in the Mogford kitchen, uniform cap tucked under an arm, his notebook in his hand. "I do 'ave to ask these questions missus," he said. Confronting Martha in her own kitchen was not a scenario he would have chosen, but duty was duty. He licked his pencil and tried again. "Young Tony Goodwin, he do live 'ere, as family?"

"You know very well he does. Come to the point. What's this nonsense all about Will? You know as much about us as we do about you." Martha said in a controlled voice.

"Right missus, like you says, but this 'ere young lad, I 'ave to know where he were last night."

"Out, he was out, he's not confined here. He goes out like any other young lad. It's always the same, give a dog a bad name, just because he had a difficult upbringing . . ."

"Ah, so he were out, I wonder where, I have to 'ave a word wi' the lad."

"For goodness sake Will, tell me what it's all about," Martha's patience was wearing thin. "Come on man, out with it. What's Tony supposed to have done?"

"Oh us a'n't accusin' anybody . . ."

"Will!"

"Oh well, there were a barn fire on a farm down

t'wards town. Us 'as to ask questions, investigate like. Now this 'ere young Tony . . ."

"Ask him yourself, he's just coming."

Tony's eyes took on a guarded look as he saw the constable. He had a mistrust of people in uniform. Not that they had all been bad to him, in fact some had helped him. It was just . . . well, uniforms meant restrictions, rules . . . institutions. He hoped that all that was in the past. He revelled in his freedom, he welcomed his obligations to the work, and to the family; he felt as if he were, at last, one of a team; and the animals, well, he loved them all, Daisy, the pigs, and that black pig down at the Sedgemore place. He didn't want anything to change, and a uniform triggered alarm bells.

"Come in lad, don't ee look so worried. It be nort but a few questions." Constable Walter smiled reassuringly. "Now, where were ee last night?"

"Out," said Tony. "Out on my bike."

"Come now lad," there was a hint of impatience in the constable's voice. "Out where?"

"I went to town."

"Yes?"

"Well, I bought a few sweets, that's all."

"An' came straight home? About what time?" The constable's pencil was poised.

"Oh I dunno, about eight."

Constable Walter turned to Martha. "The fire were spotted 'bout half seven."

"Fire, what fire?" asked Tony.

"The Sedgemore place, down towards town, the barn . . ."

"Sedgemore's barn," Tony's face paled. "The black sow, is she all right? She was just about to pig."

"She be safe, so I understands. The hay and straw were one end, she were t'other. Now, she were 'bout to pig ee says. How could ee tell; must be a bit of an expert." The constable spoke admiringly.

"Oh, it's easy," said a pleased Tony. "She had milk on her tits."

Constable Walter smiled. He knew a bit about pigs himself. "She did pig soon after they got 'er out. Now lad, ee were in that barn to see that 'er udder were drippin' milk. Us'll start again. Where were ee last night 'bout seven?"

"Well to tell the truth . . ." began Tony.

"Which be always 'elpful," said the policeman.

"I did look in just to see the old girl. She's a Large Black, and I was interested. The barn's on the roadside. I started visiting the barn one day when I stopped to talk to the children. They showed me the sow. She's a beauty, black all over."

Martha spoke up. "There you are then Will. The barn was not alight when Tony looked in. That must be helpful to your enquiries." Martha spoke dismissively, but the constable returned doggedly to his questioning.

"There were a fire near town week 'afore. Again a barn. Now lad where were ee that night?" He consulted his notebook. "Last Wednesday."

"I would be at the pictures. I often go on a Wednesday."

"And what did ee see lad?"

"I don't remember, it was boring, I came out before the end. I might remember in a minute."

"When was the fire reported Will?" asked Martha anxiously.

"'Bout ten thirty," said Will ominously. "It do look black missus, I expects I'll be back." He took his leave. "Wish it were somebody else Mrs Mogford, he do seem a likeable lad. What makes it worse, a young lad was seen riding away on a bicycle." Constable Walter mounted his bike and rode off.

Martha was worried. When Mogford came in, he got straight on the phone to Constable Walter.

He reported to Martha. "It looks bad m'dear. A

motorist was passing as the fire started. A youth on a bike came out like a bat out of hell and headed away from town. The motorist rushed to the house to raise the alarm. The Sedgemores were out, only the girls at home. They had seen nothing. The oldest was busy with homework, the two younger ones were glued to the television. The motorist phoned for the fire brigade and helped the girls to get the sow out. There was not much else to be done till the firemen arrived. Luckily the barn was down on the roadside away from the other buildings. It could have been worse, but I feel that young Tony's being a bit evasive. Where is he anyway?"

"He's up in his room," said Luke. "Can't stand the doubting looks, I shouldn't wonder. Well, I believe the boy, whatever anyone else says. It was just coincidence that he was in the barn just before the arsonist. That Will Walter ought to know the boy's telling the truth. Can't see further than his nose. I've a good mind to drop him from the cricket team."

"Hardly politic in your first year as captain. You will be hard put to it to scrape up a team come the summer; that is if you have a field to play on."

"Well, I stand by the lad, if he is being evasive he has his reasons, you'll see."

"We all stand by him," said Mogford. "He's part of the family, as it were, but the truth will come out. If there's nothing more to it, well and good, but he is behaving out of character, a bit sort of shifty about it, I think there's more, he's hiding something."

"Go and get him down Luke," said Martha. "He mustn't feel he can't go out. He saved up long enough for that bike; he's entitled to use it."

"Right," said Luke. "And I'm going to tell him we all believe in him, and just to carry on as normal. He's innocent until someone shows me something different, then I won't believe it."

A few days of awkwardness followed. Tony was

unusually subdued. He spent time in his room, and didn't go out. Constable Walter called again to go over his story, but Tony had nothing to add.

Luke was again stout in Tony's defence, extolling his many good qualities, among them a knowledge of cricket. "He learned how to play in some of those schools he's been at. Good with the bat, so I understand, could go in after you at number five; you might find yourself paired up with him."

"Well it do stand in 'is favour," admitted the constable. "He could be charged though, if nort comes up to prove 'is story."

"Then you must catch the real culprit," insisted Luke.

Constable Walter put on his cycle clips and prepared to mount. "It do look bad maister, real bad, an' him a cricketer an' all." He rode off tut tutting, and shaking his head.

* * *

Mogford meantime had visited Jim Comer at the factory. It was understood at home that some sort of a deal had been struck.

The factory would continue, at least for the time being. Mogford didn't reveal any details and nobody asked. Mogford's deals were best left to cook on a slow oven.

A week had passed since the barn fire. It was time for Hammy Second to make his last visit of the day to the great outdoors before bedding down. Martha was escorting him to a patch of grass when an unfamiliar sound assailed her ears. There was a crackling, rising and falling in volume, and then the boom of a small explosion. She rushed indoors. "There's a fire," she called.

"Not here, not our barn?" Mogford was pulling on his boots.

"No, no, not here, it sounds like nearer town, there was a sort of explosion."

"The factory, could be Jim's factory," surmised Luke.

"Those drums of beads would expand and explode. Let's go." He called up the stairs. "Tony, come quick, there's a fire in town."

"We'll all go," said Martha. "We might be able to do something."

As they approached town it was clear that it was a major fire and soon it was obvious where it was located. Down past the concrete works and the rubbish tip, it was Jim's factory, and it was well ablaze. Flames leapt high into the black sky, an exploding barrel sent a shower of sparks spiralling upwards; it was indeed a spectacle.

Three appliances were already on the scene and a small crowd had gathered. Firemen scurried hither and thither. Soon jets of water hissed at the heart of the fire, and the chief had time to explain.

"Luckily, nobody inside," he said. "Nothing much to be done, we can't save anything, and those popping barrels make it dangerous. We'll just control it, there's not much danger of it spreading. An ideal site for a fire." He grinned and bustled off about his business as Jim and Sally arrived to join the Mogfords.

"Well that's that," said Jim sorrowfully. "You know, I think I could just about have pulled it off. I suppose the insurance money will bale us out financially, but still . . ."

He was interrupted by the arrival of a police sergeant. "Well we caught the little blighter Mr Mogford. Thanks to your tip off about how inflammable this place was, we've been keeping an eye on it. The lad pedalled straight into our policeman. Caught red handed you might say, no doubt it was him, he had polystyrene beads stuck to his coat with static. Anyway he's confessed; to the others as well; lets your lad off the hook I'm pleased to say." He patted Tony on the head, touched his cap to Martha, nodded to the others, and went back to his duties.

Tony stoically suffered a bear hug from Martha, and the congratulations of the others, then a broad grin of relief spread over his face before clouding, as a thought struck him. "That other boy. He'll most likely end up in an institution," he said.

"He'll get some help I expect," suggested Luke. "Anyone who could put the black pig's life at risk needs some help, wouldn't you think?"

"I suppose so," said Tony thoughtfully, then brightened as another thought struck him. "Now I can start going out again."

Jim Comer turned to Mogford. "This puts a different complexion on our deal," he said. "There will be a bit of insurance money in the pot, instead of debts."

"We'll talk about that later," replied Mogford. "There may be some angles we haven't looked at yet. Meantime I think we should all go home."

The next morning Mogford had a long telephone conversation with Sally's father; then he arranged to meet Sally and Jim in a pub. When he came home he was looking rather pleased with himself.

The family were grouped around the Aga with mugs of bedtime drinks. Tony had come in five minutes earlier. He too looked well pleased with life.

"Some people are never home," said Luke to his mother. "These two, and even Daisy the other day."

"Daisy, what on earth . . ." Martha was lost for words.

"It slipped my mind; but remember that day she was hollering; the day before the inseminator came?"

There were nods all round.

"Go on," urged Mogford. "What's she been up to?"

"Up to the Hall it seems. You remember Ma' she was late appearing for afternoon milking. Well, she had taken a walk; trespassing in fact. Colonel Fortescue told me all about it this morning."

"Go on Luke," said Martha. "You *are* exasperating, all about what?"

"Well it seems she got into one of his fields, where his Aberdeen Angus herd grazes, and – there's a very fine prize winning bull running with the cows."

"Ah," said Martha. "I begin to see. Did she . . .?"

"'Fraid so," grinned Luke. "But the Major was happy enough about it. 'Give the little beggar some exercise,' was what he said. He was referring to the bull of course."

There was a small smile of quiet satisfaction on Martha's face. "It's like I've always said . . ." she began, then stopped. Perhaps this was not the right time to mention bottled sperm. "Well anyway, we should have a black calf to look forward to."

"Or a Jersey if the insemination took," suggested Mogford. "Or nothing even."

But Martha had already made up her mind; she was quite sure Daisy would have a black calf.

"Have you some news for us Da'?" Asked Luke.

Mogford looked at the clock. "Yes," he said. "But I vote we sleep on it. It'll give us something to talk about at breakfast."

* * *

"Come on then Da', tell us all about it. Tony and I will soon be getting back to work." Luke's patience was being sorely tried by his father's leisurely enjoyment of his breakfast.

"You know your Da' Luke. He has to make a big mystery of everything." Martha rounded on Mogford. "Mogford," she said sharply. "We're all waiting."

"Oh, right m'dear," Mogford pushed his plate away. "Now what was it you wanted to know?"

"Mogford," there was more than a hint of exasperation in Martha's voice. "Jim Comer, what have you arranged?"

Mogford beamed. "We had this deal."

"Perhaps you had better tell us about that for a start off," suggested Martha.

"Right m'dear. It was like this. Jim was up against it. Customers were slow to pay. He was hard put to it to pay for raw materials, and suppliers were holding back on deliveries. He had nothing in the bank to cushion this state of affairs. The bank wouldn't help and without the raw beads he could not produce; therefore nothing to sell, and soon, no customers. That's the way I saw it and I thought, well, we had done very well with our calves, there was a bit in the bank, I put up enough to ensure supplies of beads for three months. He had three months to concentrate on getting his business off the ground; then we'd see."

"This was a loan, Mogford?" asked Martha.

"A loan," agreed Mogford. "But unsecured. The deal was, if he made a go of it, he would pay me back eventually at a better than normal rate of interest. If he didn't, it was an interest free loan, to be paid back sometime. We shook hands on it. At the time it looked as if he was swimming against the tide; no more than holding his own."

"And now," suggested Luke, "there's the insurance money."

"Yes," agreed Mogford. "Luckily he had good cover. There will be enough to take care of everything, including the loan."

"With substantial interest," grinned Luke.

"As you say," said Mogford. "But in fact I don't intend to collect the interest or even all of the loan."

"But Mogford," protested Martha, "we're not *that* flush at the bank, and we may fall on hard times ourselves."

Mogford held up a hand. "Hear me out m'dear. I had a long talk with Sally's father. I felt he needed to be reminded of his duties, with a grandchild due any minute."

"I've had thoughts along those lines," agreed Martha.

"Quite. Well he has a cottage which Sally and Jim can rent. Jim will have a job on the farm for a start, and he can have the use of an empty building for some part time moulding work, to see if he can build up a business."

"A bit like our hessian gloves," said Martha.

"Well, a bit, but I have suggested he does some thorough research. There must be a specialist area. Moulds that don't lend themselves to mass production. The quality, expensive side. Anyway he can work in gradually, with his bread and butter secure."

"And your investment?" queried Martha.

"Oh, that, part of that buys Luke a small share of the business. I'm sure Jim's going to need a bit of advice on the machinery side."

Luke taken by surprise, could only stare, and before he could speak, Mogford turned his attention to Tony. "Now, young Tony, tell me, what's this fascination with that black pig of Sedgemore's?"

"Well I sort of advise them. They don't know much about pigs; it's a bit of a hobby with them. He pushed back his chair. I think I had better get back to work." A flush was beginning to colour his cheeks as he rose hurriedly and left.

"Was it something I said?" asked Mogford.

Luke was grinning hugely. "The Sedgemore pig is a sensitive area. I've been asking a few questions. The eldest of the Sedgemore girls is fifteen. It started when she asked Tony into the barn to see the black sow; then she started bringing her homework down to the barn, and they would work on it together. Our Tony, it seems, is in love."

"Well it was nice of Tony to help the girl with her homework," said Martha, a little stiffly. She was not at all sure that she approved of this latest development.

"Ah," said Luke. "It wasn't that way round; this is apparently a very bright girl; there are gaps in our Tony's education."

"The poor lamb," exclaimed Martha. "I didn't realise, and me an ex-teacher; I could help him fill those gaps."

"Not quite the same thing, m'dear," said Mogford gently. "Not quite the same at all."

17
All's fair

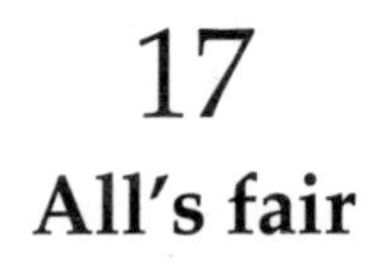

"IT's always the same," complained Martha. "Every time I'm busy and want to get on after lunch, you men sit around and talk. Why you couldn't chat at breakfast like you usually do, I don't know."

"Well, you said you were busy then too," said Mogford reasonably. "Anyway one of the things we want to discuss affects Tony. If he's old enough to go courting, I reckon he's old enough for a bit of responsibility."

"Maybe I'd better go, like Mrs Mogford says." The tell tale colour was creeping up Tony's cheeks.

"No, no, you stay. Anything we plan is for your ears as well. You're part of the team you know. I might even say an important part of the team, and now you're courting . . ."

"Well I'm not, Mr Mogford, at least, not properly. I meet her inside the cinema. I can't afford to do anything else."

Luke chortled. "That's the way we all start Tony, but we ought to look at your money. Just you stay and listen."

Martha snorted and set about her chores. "Well if it affects Tony you had better get on with it," she said grudgingly. "I hear, Luke, that Samantha's due a visit."

"Arrives Thursday, should see her on Friday morning," said Luke amiably.

"Well don't get carried away," grumbled Martha.

"You're not a free agent any more. Anyway, get on with that business and let me get on with my work."

"Well," said Mogford. "I've just completed a deal which gives us ten acres of land just west of the village. We could increase the flock. I thought we might establish a proper flock, of say, Half Breds, or Cluns, instead of the oddments I pick up around the markets. What do you think?"

"That we're getting more and more legit, by the day," grinned Luke.

"So you're in favour. And you Tony?"

"I'd like to learn more about the sheep," agreed Tony.

"And you m'dear?"

"Hmph!" snorted Martha. "I can tell it's spring. It's not only the plants that feel the sap rising. I would be outnumbered anyway," she said ungraciously.

"Now the other matter might concern Tony when he's a bit older. I know he's old enough to . . ." Mogford caught Martha's eye and changed tack. "But of course he's too young for what I plan at the moment which involves a lorry."

Tony's eyes sparkled. "A lorry, that would be great."

"Well here's my thinking on it. Up country they burn acres of straw, down here we buy it. I was thinking of a merchanting operation; fill a need; something for Tony to run later on."

"Well," said Luke with uncharacteristic caution, "we'd have to invest in a lorry, secondhand perhaps. I could keep it running. We'd have to take account of depreciation, and a full 'C' licence. Farmers' Goods and Private wouldn't cover it. Then fuel; would the lorry have work every day . . .?"

Mogford looked at his son with a new respect. "Well said, Luke. Good points. We would have to keep the capital cost down to a minimum, maybe license the lorry for the season only. Anyway I want Tony and you to think about it. Work out some figures; and talking about working out, when does that arm wrestling contest take place in the pub?"

"It's next month," said Luke. "I haven't had much practice. How would you like to be my trainer, Tony?"

"That would be great," enthused Tony. "They tell me that Duke chap is strong opposition."

"Duke?" queried Mogford. "I don't think I know this Duke. Who is he Luke?"

"Oh, he's an odd sort of a chap. Lives in town and seems to have a mission in life to visit as many village dances as possible. This means we don't see him very often as he travels his district."

"A bit of a ladies' man, by the sound of it," suggested Mogford.

"I don't really know," said Luke. "As far as I know he hasn't left his mark anywhere."

"We'll have none of that talk at the table please," snapped Martha. "Anyway I heard a little bit about him, from Rosie at the pub. Well built chap; a coalman; he delivers to a few houses in the village."

"Well done Ma, good job some of us keep our ears to the ground, but there's more. He's a coalman by day, black as the Earl of Hell's waistcoat, by all accounts, and inclined to sing at the top of his voice as he drives along. A bit of an extrovert. But that all changes in the evening. At a dance he looks like a tailor's dummy. Pencil line moustache, sharp suit, tie with jewelled pin, about two inches of cuffs, and cufflinks that dazzle, and a cigarette delicately held. Oh, and he must have a good scrub because he is pink and white, not a trace of coal dust. And his hair; middle parting and plastered down."

"Sounds like a real dude," said Mogford. "What about the nickname, Duke, how did he come by that?"

"Well," Luke was warming to his subject. "It's his attitude. He's so affected, handkerchief up the sleeve, drinks gin and tonic, doesn't fraternise, just stands about looking elegant."

"But he's strong, so I hear," said Tony. "Folk think he might beat you Luke. I think I'll start you training tonight."

"Why did I open my big mouth," groaned Luke. "Now I have a trainer who's going to make me work."

"Which is what you should all be about," said Martha tartly. "Now, all of you, out of my kitchen."

* * *

Luke was grooming Major Fortescue's latest acquisition, a tall bay four year old, when he heard her. 'Heathcliff . . . Heathcliff.'

He shambled to the door, grinning, and pulling his forelock, "'Ere m'lady," he called, and then she was standing there, in the doorway, eyes sparkling, smiling, as beautiful and graceful as a spring flower. It was the Samantha of old, but with a new air of worldliness, and when she spoke, there was just a hint of a transatlantic drawl.

"Really Luke, if you had only read the book, you could have improved on that. We should be free spirits, rushing across a bleak moor to clasp each other with fire and passion."

"Oh, that," grinned Luke. "It only gives you indigestion. Anyway, how about a big hello kiss?" He clutched her to him and planted a large kiss.

"Luke," she protested. "You have stable muck and hayseeds all down your front."

"No more than you . . . now. Come and see the horses. Maybe we could go for a ride; I have to exercise this big lad anyway."

Samantha ran an expert eye over the bay. "This must be the one Dad's been talking about. Seventeen and a half hands; a real weight carrier."

"That's right," said Luke proudly. "A horse fit for a cavalry officer, big and strong, and a bit spirited. Needs to be exercised regularly."

"So," said Samantha admiringly. "You've moved up from the old piebald to this?"

"Yes," said Luke modestly. "As far as the horses go, I can hold my own with any man . . . or woman." He smiled at Samantha and his eyes were warm. "I reckon it was all physical with us," he said softly.

"It still is, as far as I'm concerned, and all's fair in love and war," she replied. "You have been warned, but come on now, let's saddle up, I want to see what you can do on a horse . . . in the first place."

"I don't think my mother would agree with you . . . about love and war. The way she sees it I'm as good as married to Betty."

They had set off walking and chatting, but the bay was restive, eyes a little wild, and spooking at anything that moved.

"I'd better gallop him," said Luke. "Get some of his nonsense out of his head."

"Right," said Samantha, when they had mounted. "Across this field, over that scrubby hedge, across the next field, and through the hunting gate into the woods." With a whoop she was off with the bay in pursuit.

There was no way Luke could hold him back. Could he jump? He had no idea. He would soon find out. The hedge was low, and by no means dense. On the other side was a shallow dry ditch. Samantha was up and over, galloping on, looking back.

It should be an easy jump. Luke leaned forward to compensate for the rise. "Hup," he shouted and loosed the reins. The bay took no notice. Powerfully he charged through the hedge, broke his stride as he scrambled through the ditch, and deposited the out of balance Luke in the cow pasture.

Samantha quickly sized up the situation, caught the loose horse, and returned to find Luke sitting up and clutching his shoulder. "Collar bone," she surmised. "Come on I'll get you up in front of me. We're not so high as that brute, and anyway, I'll be able to cuddle you all the way home."

"So much for the passion," grumbled Luke. "At least Heathcliff had the good sense to run about the moor on foot."

Samantha insisted on a visit to the hospital where no broken bones were found, only bruising, but they supplied a light sling for support. Samantha drove him home. "I won't come in," she said. "There's a strange car. You have visitors."

Luke entered the kitchen. At first he didn't see her, but she crossed the kitchen floor in a rush of steps. Her arms were round him. He was being embraced from top to toe with his damaged shoulder carefully outside. It was an embrace of passion, physical, a heady contact from clinging lips downwards. "We heard about your accident, they phoned from the Hall," Betty whispered between kisses.

"Betty," he finally managed to gasp. "I didn't know."

"It was your Mum's idea. Thought I needed a break."

"I think we need to be married," whispered Luke hoarsely.

"I think I need a ring on my finger, at least," replied Betty. "And I would like to be sure you didn't still have one in your nose; except of course when you come up to London."

Martha, who had tactfully withdrawn, bustled noisily through the inner door. "Why don't you two take a holiday together this summer?" she suggested.

"Mother, and us not married."

"Everybody's doing it these days," said Martha, her voice gruff with embarrassment. "You are going to be married?"

Martha was answered by the love light in their eyes. She would one day gain a daughter. She was delighted at the prospect.

Later Luke caught his mum on her own. "Well organised Ma," he said.

"Oh, I thought it would be nice," said Martha innocently. "How was Samantha?"

"Oh fine, just fine, looking like a million dollars. She said something to me. I didn't think you'd approve."

"Really? Tell me."

"She said – 'All's fair in love and war.' "

Martha smiled, a secret little smile. "My sentiments exactly," she said.

* * *

Luke shouldered his way through the throng, Tony following in his wake.

The arm wrestling contest was a great crowd puller; a bonanza night for the landlord, and a busy one for himself, his wife and Rosie, the recently arrived barmaid.

"Just a half for Luke," said Tony firmly. "And I mean that. He'll have to be at his best to beat this Duke chap."

"That's him over there," Rosie indicated. Duke stood, aloof, immaculate, dandified, a small glass in one hand, a cigarette in an elegant holder, in the other.

"I've been watching him," said Rosie. "Looks like a real gent."

"Fancy him?" grinned Luke.

"You could say that," said Rosie. "Not as much as I fancy you, of course, but then, you're not in the market any more."

Impatient calls further along the bar had her hurrying off.

"Just the one half, Luke," said Tony sternly.

Luke sighed. There had been times during the last few weeks when he had regretted appointing Tony as his trainer. That apparatus he had rigged up in the barn; a pulley, a weight on the end of a rope, and a hand hold, set at just the right angle; an hour every day, practising, with Tony increasing the weight at intervals. Still it had made a difference. He was able to shift more weight now, he could hold the weight stationary for quite a long time. As

Tony said, 'It might come down to who could hold on the longest.'

"Cheers," he said, raising his half pint. "I'd better make it last."

"Cheers," replied Tony. "And you can have as much as you want after the final."

They sipped quietly for a moment, taking stock of the room. A table and two chairs occupied centre stage. Here the semi-finals would be held and later, the final.

The landlord had prudently settled the earlier rounds during the week. A pall of tobacco smoke drifted up to hang below the low ceiling, dimming the lights. There was excitement in the air, in anticipation of the titan struggles about to take place. A few bets were covertly offered and taken.

The room was packed to the corners, except for the one where Duke stood. It was as if they sensed a brooding menace in the disdainful posture, the aloof, almost contemptuous dismissal of those around him.

He was obviously well built, and much fancied to win. A close observer might have noticed that the eyes beneath the lowered lids, often strayed in Rosie's direction.

Rosie for her part was intrigued. She was not unaware that the anatomy she presented above the bar was appreciated by the clientele, especially when she leaned forward to exchange confidences. She found occasion to lean forward from time to time within the range of Duke's vision. She liked men; not all men, just the nice ones, and especially if they were well built. Duke was well built, well dressed, he was different, an enigma. Rosie's curiosity was aroused.

Blackie was announcing the semi-finalists. Luke had drawn a tough Irishman, one of a gang of navvies digging drains in the area. Duke was to wrestle with the Irishman's brother in the first semi-final.

The Irishman prepared to lower his untidy bulk into

one of the chairs but paused and slowly rolled up a sleeve to expose a sinewy arm well layered with hard muscle. A diet of ditch digging and heavy drinking tended to produce weight and muscle, and, this early in the evening, an amiable temperament. The grin he directed towards Duke was tolerant and amused.

Blackie was doing the honours. "On my right is . . ." He turned to the Irishman for help.

"Paddy, sure now aren't we all called Paddy." His grin widened.

"Paddy," said Blackie.

There was a cheer from the man's brother and a group of hardy ditch diggers who were having the time of their lives.

"An' may I introduce the Duke," went on Blackie.

"Geez," said the Irishman. "Nobody said I was to wrestle with a titled gent, and me hand so rough wi' all that low grade labouring work."

He held out his hand. Duke ignored it.

"Sit ee down, you Irish bastard," he suggested uncivilly. "Us is 'ere to wrestle, so zip up that great quarry hole an' get on wi' it." Duke's accent belied his upper crust bearing and brought forth a cheer from the locals.

Paddy's amiability, transient at the best of times had evaporated; the group of navvies moved closer. There was a hint of menace in the movement of the non-smiling faces.

Blackie's patience was being sorely tried. "Sit ee down, both on ee or I might sort ee both out." There were nods and smiles from people in the crowd. In his forge days Blackie was unbeatable, but that was a few years ago now.

"Y'er jacket Duke," he suggested.

Duke looked surprised. "It be hardly worth takin' it off. I don't expect to be more'n a minute."

This brought forth a loud growling sound from the

navvies followed by shouted advice to Paddy on how to handle the cocky toff.

Indeed it took less than a minute. The infuriated Irishman put his all into an initial assault and failed to move the rock-like Duke. A swift counter attack from Duke finished the contest.

Blackie was about to introduce Luke's opponent. "I suppose ee is called Paddy as well," he said.

"To be sure," said the Irishman. "An' all they over there, all the lot o' them. Sure now it's like this. Say we were to start some trouble." He paused significantly. "The 'polis' would have trouble deciding which Paddy started it. Either we'd all end up in a cell or none of us. You see what I mean?"

Constable Walter standing nearby thought he understood well enough. Some of his superiors might have described it as a volatile situation. It was a good job he was off duty and wearing civvies. Perhaps he would leave early anyway, he was feeling a bit tired.

Luke, on his trainer's advice, went for the swift kill and moved Paddy's arm about six inches. Fighting back from his position took its toll and Luke succeeded with a second thrust.

The final proved to be a stiffer test. After five minutes the hands were still locked in the upright position. Blackie called a break.

"A draw so far lads, get ee a drink an' a bit of a rest an' come back in ten minutes."

Luke had a small sip from his half pint and surveyed the scene. It was worrying. The navvies were in a tactical huddle in a corner. Luke was in no doubt that Duke was to be punished for his insulting remarks. Duke himself was making use of the time to further his cause with Rosie. Rosie, elbows on the bar, was displaying for his exclusive benefit. He had made progress to the extent of buying her a drink, but his eyes strayed towards the Irish contingent from time to time.

Luke knew he was sizing up the odds which were far from favourable. He summoned Rosie. "Top up this for me," he said, "and let me whisper in your ear."

Just before being called to the table Luke gave Tony two small commissions.

"Right lads," said Blackie. "Us'll try to get a result."

As they settled Luke leaned forward and whispered urgently in Duke's ear.

"Just telling him what a prat he is," grinned Luke to the crowding in Irish contingent.

They grinned. "Hurry it up then lad," said one of their number. "Sure now we have ideas about walking his lordship home."

"When I've finished with him, all in good time." Luke smiled disarmingly.

The contest had reached another impasse. Neither would give an inch. Then suddenly, with an ear splitting 'Geronimo' Duke broke off, leapt over the bar and disappeared through a rear door.

The Irishmen rushed for the street door. It was locked. They poured over the bar and through the rear door. There was the sound of a car starting up and roaring off. The strains of 'Danny Boy', badly sung, drifted back in the night air.

* * *

"Just as I was getting to know him," bemoaned Rosie. It was a week later. Tony and Luke had been passing and decided to call for a lunchtime drink.

"After all I have some catching up to do," Luke had complained.

Tony was well pleased with the result of the match. A draw had been officially declared. At least that's what Blackie had said and who was going to argue.

"One or two things puzzle me still," Rosie was talking again. "I know what you told me to do – open all the doors, point the way for Duke, but the key for the front door, that was in the landlord's pocket."

"That was Tony's contribution, part of his early training. He helped himself to the landlord's key, and slipped my car key in Duke's pocket. All I had to do was whisper, there's a car key in your right hand jacket pocket, an A40 van out front, the street door is locked, Rosie will see you through the back. When you're ready, over the bar and out the back." Luke grinned, "I said something else too."

"What was that?" asked Rosie.

"I said, Rosie fancies you."

The landlord had arrived behind the bar in time to hear the explanation. "Well Luke, you and Tony saved a reconstruction of the Battle of the Boyne here, I'm grateful to you. Drinks on the house. Oh and you might get a chance to meet Duke again. He's delivering coal, could be here any minute.You got your van back all right?"

Luke grinned. "With a bag of coal in the back as a thank you."

Tony was raising a well topped pint. The landlord, on special occasions, was inclined to ignore his tender years and was about to move to the rear when the uneven beat of a lorry could be heard outside.

"Sounds a bit rough," said Luke.

"So is the singing, I don't know which is the roughest," said Tony.

Indeed 'The Rose of Tralee' could have been sung better, but perhaps not any louder. As the engine cut, so that notes died away and the sound of the footsteps and the crash of disgorged coal indicated unloading. Presently Duke presented himself in the bar. His shirt was collarless, his trousers baggy, a cap clung to the back of his head and the whole was covered in a film of black coal dust. Through this a cheerful grin split his face.

"Ten bags landlord," he said cheerfully. "Thirsty work."

"Have a drink," suggested the landlord.

"Well," said Duke doubtfully, "I don't usually like to drink on an empty stomach."

"Ah," the landlord was catching on. "Later then; Rosie take Duke through the back and get him something to eat. Oh," he called after them. "Better put some newspapers down for Duke to sit on."

There was the sound of a kettle being filled, cupboard doors opened and shut, dishes clattered, there was the muted sound of conversation and then a scuffle and a piercing shriek.

Duke appeared, running fast. He didn't stop to lift the bar flap but vaulted over. In hot pursuit came Rosie wielding a broom. She was black from the face downwards with black handprints on the back of her partly unzipped dress.

"Don't show your face here again you black devil," she shouted.

But Duke was in his cab, the engine fired and a raucous rendering of 'Sweet Rosie O'Grady' drifted mockingly back with the exhaust smoke.

Luke grinned at Tony. "I think you could say Duke left his mark," he said.

"Or maybe, as your mother might say, all's fair . . ." Tony stopped. He still felt uncomfortable articulating words like 'love' out loud, in broad daylight. It was different in the cinema, in the warm darkness, holding hands, whispering . . .

18
Elephant synod

"THAT was good news about Daisy this morning, don't you think?" Mountfield had called in the morning to perform a pregnancy diagnosis.

Martha smiled, recalling his words. 'Just the size of a cricket ball,' he had said. 'Definitely in calf for the autumn.' He had then gone on to talk about the proposed visit, later in the summer, from the County cricket team. Everyone apparently had confidence in Mogford's ability to conjure up a new ground. The long standing arrangement with the county had not been cancelled.

Martha wondered if at another time the foetus might have been the size of an orange, but the main thing was Daisy was in calf, her future secured for another lactation. Martha was sure the calf would be black like its father. She had no time for the tube of the inseminator. It would definitely be half Aberdeen Angus.

"Don't you agree?" she insisted, her tone a little sharper. Hammy Second assumed a sitting position and tilted his head.

"That's better," said Martha. "Now I can tell you a bit about Luke and Betty going on holiday. Isn't it exciting, they are going to Africa, to see the wild animals." This was indeed exciting news, which brought a small yelp from Hammy Second.

"Good, I can see you are getting interested."

Hammy Second attempted a tail wag while still in the sitting position.

"Now, I expect you think they are going to Kenya like everybody else. Well you are quite wrong. They are going to a place called Zambia, and will visit a game park near a big river called the Kafue." Martha giggled. "None of us knew where it was. We had to look it up in an atlas. Now isn't that exciting?"

Hammy Second was on his feet wagging his tail wildly. Not only was Martha's obvious excitement infectious, she was getting the biscuit tin down from the shelf.

* * *

The take-off was a little bumpy.

"You know," said Luke. "I was a bit surprised I had to help you sort out your seat belt. Anyone would think it was your first flight."

"It is," said Betty shortly. "And I don't like these air pockets, it upsets my stomach, and doesn't do much for my nerves either. I expect you're a veteran of at least one flight?"

"Not so. The highest I get off the ground is on that seventeen and a half hands charger of Colonel Fortescue's. Even then I'm capable of falling off. No, this is a first for both of us. Look at all the lights down below. Aren't you glad we are flying at night?"

"We're flying at night because it's cheaper, and I don't want to look. Perhaps later. How long is the flight?"

"Only about eleven hours," said Luke cheerfully. "You'll have time to get used to it."

Food arrived, and soon alpine peaks began to pass below them, stark and clear in the moonlight. Betty chanced a look downwards and was enchanted with the sight of villages and townships far below. Lights twinkled like jewels in folds of the mountains. A fairytale world. Airborne again after a stop in Rome and then, the boot leg of Italy, just like it was on a map, and at some point they fell asleep, tucked in, under a blanket and close together.

When they awoke, a brilliant sun filled the cabin with its light. The sky was a startling blue, and below they could see clouds like balls of cottonwool. Through gaps they could see the endless rolling dunes of the Sahara desert.

Betty's fear had receded as excitement and interest took over. So much that was new and different from the world they had so recently left. The Sahara seemed endless, but eventually the sand gave way to scrub trees and grass and small clusters of thatched homes of sticks and mud, and then hours later, the airport, and the bus into the capital city. The drive offered more new sights. A woman carrying a large basket of eggs on her head, attracted Luke's attention. "We're going to learn something here," he said.

"Don't get ideas," laughed Betty. "Look at that one." A woman carrying a box of matches and a packet of cigarettes on her head was the object of their interest.

A meal in town and a hired car, and the adventure had started. The game park rondavels hove into view like an oasis after a dusty drive on dirt roads, through townships reminiscent of the wild west of America and a quick spray and inspection at the park entrance.

"Tsetse fly precautions," explained Luke.

They were met by a young man in shorts and a hat with a mock leopardskin head band.

"I'm Christie, the camp warden," he said. "Let me show you round. It's a small camp. There is a bigger one, with a restaurant and a swimming pool, but you'll see as much game here, and we have a sing-song round the camp fire after dark."

"Have you many people in?" asked Luke.

"Ten apart from yourselves. All nationalities. Two Scottish ladies, they're a bit of a handful, giving me a bit of stick. Middle aged widows, on a once in a lifetime holiday and determined to make the most of it. Anyway let me show you round. You've brought food?"

"Yes, supplies for a week, and cameras, shorts and floppy hats," grinned Luke.

"Right, you may need thick socks if we go on foot safari. Cookhouse over there. You have been allocated a fridge and a store cupboard. Just give the cook your meat and whatever in the morning and he will cook your evening meal. There are cooking facilities in the rondavels as well. Come and meet the others at the camp fire later."

The rondavels were comfortable, if basic, and mosquito nets draped the single beds.

"You can see why we needed to take those malaria pills, this place must be an insect's paradise," commented Luke.

"Not to mention all the other prods and jabs we endured," smiled Betty. "But it was worth all the pain. Just think Luke, tonight, lying under the thin gauze of our mosquito nets . . ."

"Or net," interjected Luke.

"As I was saying . . . with the insects buzzing outside, and thinking about tomorrow and all the animals we will see. Shall we just try the nets for size? It'll be another new experience."

"I have a better idea," said Luke. "Let's try one of the nets now, and leave the other for later." He held out a hand. "Talking of new experiences . . ."

It was some hours later before they joined the others at the camp fire. Somewhere by the river an animal grunted, loud in the still night air.

"Hippo," said Christie briefly.

"Farting," said a stout lady seated near him.

"That's not quite accurate Meg," said another middle aged lady of similar build. "It's belching. It's all that grass they gobble down at night."

The warden sighed. "Come and meet everybody. This is Meg and her friend Mary. They are good singers and they argue a lot." The introductions continued and then Christie suggested a song. "No hymns tonight, we'll save those for Sunday. Anything else?" He directed his most severe look at the two stout ladies. "I know you both sing in a choir, but . . ." He broke off as a thought struck him. "Tell you what, if you ever find yourself surrounded by elephants, try a few of your hymns on them. It's supposed to have a calming effect."

"Humph," snorted Meg. "I don't think you have any elephants in this park. We haven't seen any yet."

"You will before the week's out. Now what was that song about the bonny banks of loch something or other?"

The ladies glared, but struck up, and soon the singsong was in full swing. The two stout ladies sang well, and with considerable power.

Betty was glad of the volume. The night noises; the shrieks of hyenas, the rasping growl of a hunting leopard, the mighty roar of a lion, and hippo noises from the river, seemed too close for comfort. She was aware of her unprotected back, exposed to the blackness behind. Her thoughts turned sleepily to a cot, a mosquito net, and a strong arm to make her feel safe.

They rose early to watch the sun rise. At first a roseate glow in the eastern sky, then an orange rim, edging upwards to sit on the horizon. An orange ball now, casting streaks of flame across the arc of the sky. Soon it was riding high, free of the earth's curve, untrammelled and climbing steadily, shedding warmth and light across the land.

The bush was coming alive, as the day feeders, apart from the unlucky ones who had been taken by the night prowlers, prepared to feed and drink.

"I didn't think anything could be so beautiful," said Betty, leaning close. The sun had not yet quite dispersed the night chill.

"You said something like that about the sunset last night," Luke reminded her.

Betty snuggled closer. "Everything had a sort of glow last night. Everything was beautiful, I hope you haven't forgotten."

"I don't think I'll ever forget last night," said Luke

seriously. "Now, what about these shorts, don't you think they're a bit short?" He grinned. "Will I get past those two Scottish ladies, do you think?"

"Well they do rib Christie about his shorts, but you have better thighs. Anyway short shorts are in fashion, and luckily you have a bit of a tan. All that rescuing of pretty girls down on the beach, I shouldn't wonder. Anyway I had better get you some breakfast, I don't want you weakening on me."

"And then the game viewing, I can hardly wait. Come on, we'll get breakfast together." He picked her up. "About time I carried you over the threshold."

"You'll soon be doing it for real," said Betty. "That is if we have a threshold."

"I'm getting a few thresholds organised for you to take a look at. Now, breakfast, and perhaps we ought to take a look at our snake bite kit."

Betty shivered.

"You don't care for snakes?" said Luke.

"It's not so much the snakes. I've seen the length of the needle in that snake kit."

Days of game viewing followed. Leaping impalas, water buck and zebras, buffalo glowering, giraffe undulating gracefully, a pride of lions resting full bellied in the shade and with great good fortune, a leopard with its prey in the fork of a tree. This and more filled their eyes and kept the cameras popping, but elephants were few and far between.

This brought a complaint from the two widows one evening at the camp fire gathering. "We haven't seen a herd of elephants close up and our holiday is nearly over," complained Meg.

"I agree with my friend . . . for once," said Mary firmly. "We want some good photos, close up, so you had better stir your stumps tomorrow."

"Oh Mary, not stumps. He's got quite shapely legs. A bit thinner than Luke's maybe, but still . . ."

"All right, all right, let's talk about tomorrow," Christie quickly changed the subject. "I was thinking about taking out a foot safari tomorrow, I wondered if you two ladies might prefer to go for a little drive on your own?"

"Why," demanded Meg, "because we're too fat?"

"Or too old?" challenged Mary.

"No, nothing like that, honest," said Christie. "It's just that, it's well, a bit strenuous, you might find it a bit tiring, and of course there's always the chance of finding yourself face to face with a rhino, or a lion that hasn't eaten for a few days. Of course I'll have my gun, nothing to worry about really, except perhaps if you step on a puff adder."

"That does it," said Meg, "We'll go and look for elephants on our own."

Christie saw them off the next morning. "You'll be perfectly safe just as long as you stay in the car. This track runs due south for fifty miles; don't leave it or you'll get lost. I'm sure you'll see elephants. If you meet them on the road, back off. If you get in any kind of trouble, sing some of your hymns."

Meg gave him a searching look. Was he having them on? But no, he seemed quite serious; indeed he appeared to be genuinely concerned for their welfare.

* * *

They had been driving through sparse bush for some time, when a clump of tallish trees invited them into its shade, some thirty yards off the road.

"Just the place for our packed lunch," said Meg.

"But it's off the road, Christie said . . ." protested Mary.

"What the eye doesn't see . . ." said Meg, and headed for the trees.

In the sudden gloom, they were unaware at first, that they were not alone. Others had sought shelter from the midday sun. As their eyes attuned to the light, they could see tall grey shapes among the trees, shapes which approached and surrounded the car, with swaying trunks and flapping ears.

An old female raised her trunk and trumpeted, a chilling sound, but they seemed more curious than disturbed.

"That will be the old matriarch," whispered Meg. "She's the leader; I wish we weren't so low down."

"Yes," agreed Mary, "it would be more bearable in a Range Rover. What shall we do?"

"Sing," said Meg. "That's what Christie said. We'll sing as loud as we can."

"Right," said Mary. "How about 'Rock of Ages'."

And that's where Christie and Luke found them, three hours later. Having finished the foot safari, Christie had suggested that they might check up on the two ladies, while Betty and the rest of the company rested, after the excitement and fatigue of foot slogging in the hot sunshine.

Cruising quietly, Christie's highly sensitive ears had picked up what sounded like a full choir performing in the trees. Approaching quietly on foot, they witnessed the spectacle of two stout ladies in their small car, giving a recital their choral society would have been proud of, to a posse of elephants, standing solemnly, like clergy at a synod, and apparently enjoying the performance.

A shot in the air told the elephants it was time to leave, and the ladies that rescue was at hand.

Peering anxiously, they saw the two men, tanned and muscular in their heavy socks and short shorts, their wide brimmed hats with imitation leopardskin hat bands giving a Hollywood flavour to the rescue.

"It was like a film," said Meg afterwards.

"I think they were a bit embarrassed – you know – with all that hugging and kissing we gave them," said Mary.

Meg chuckled, "I expect they'll leave that bit out when they tell the story round the camp fire."

* * *

The sun was up and the car was loaded. The two ladies were about to leave. Christie was fussing around. "You're sure you have all you need? You know the way? Plenty to drink?" And then unexpectedly he hugged them both in turn. "I shall miss you two ladies, that's for sure, you've been great."

"What a bear hug," said Meg getting into the car.

Mary sighed, "One for the road, you could say, now it's back to the real world."

The car rolled forward on the dirt road and picked up speed, the dust cloud billowed and a robust musical rendering drifted back.

As distance began to swallow up the sound, Christie, Luke and Betty and an assorted group of well-wishers could just make out the words. 'We're no' awa' tae bide awa',' then the car sped round a bend, and the dust began to settle.

Back in the rondavel for breakfast, Betty sighed. "In a few days it will be our turn."

"Well," said Luke cheerfully, "it seems you get to hug the game warden."

"Talking of hugging," said Betty thoughtfully, "I vote we have a day on our own. Go and look for elephants. Find a nice shady spot for lunch. The elephants may come to see what we are getting up to."

Luke grinned. "Just as long as you don't expect me to sing."

The days passed quickly and soon they were watching the last sunset of their holiday; the sky shot brilliantly with red and gold, the fiery orb of the sun dropping swiftly into its slot behind the horizon, the colour fading, then the darkness.

Some time in the night, Betty awoke. Deep in the bush a drumbeat pulsed its throbbing rhythm. A lion roared, and the moonlit night was filled with sounds. The carnivores were abroad. Betty shivered. This was nature in the raw, primitive, elemental.

She turned her thoughts homeward. The farm; the village; she would be down there for the cricket match, and then again for that other function. Perhaps they would need a marquee; how many bridesmaids? How many guests . . .? Thoughts drifted pleasantly through her mind, her eyes closed, her sleep was untroubled.

19

What falls to the floor

"IF I could get a word in," said Mogford pointedly.

Luke paused in mid-sentence. "Sorry Da' am I talking too much again?"

"Well let's put it this way," said Mogford. "For the last three breakfast times I've been wanting to tell you all about the cricket pitch, and also, it'll be harvest time before we know where we are, and there's the hay and straw business to finalise, so, if we could leave the African continent just where it is this morning, we could talk business; and I really would like to explain about the cricket field."

"And there's the wedding," chipped in Martha. "Guest lists, catering, clothes, there's a lot to see to. And a place for the young couple to set up house."

"Yes m'dear. Luke and Betty have been looking."

"Near town Ma, so Betty can perhaps carry on teaching. We'll take you to see it soon."

"Well I suppose she could get a job till the children come along," mused Martha.

Mogford sighed. He was being side-tracked again. "First, the cricket match," he said firmly. "We do still have a fixture?"

"Oh yes Da'. It's a long standing arrangement. It was never cancelled. Everyone was confident you'd come up with something. I'm surprised you have had no news for us before this."

Mogford groaned. "If everybody keeps quiet, I'll tell you now. You all know that field I bought near the village, to make space for a better sheep flock. Well unless there's strong family objections, I want to give it to the village. It's flat and was seeded down about three years ago with a good grass mixture. There's time to make a wicket and sort out a pavilion . . ."

"Da', hold on, can we afford it. I mean, give away land, the freehold. And what about the flock?" Luke was taken aback; this was serious, this was now; lingering memories of the African adventure gave way to current worries.

"I'm sure your Dad knows what he's about, Luke. There must be more to it."

"Well, there is m'dear, as you say. I had a good deal on part of the old cricket ground."

"Ah," said Martha. "I thought there was more to it. Go on Mogford."

"Well, when I first got wind of the new road proposal, I was sure there was only one sensible way for it to go; through the cricket field. I got in touch with the absent owner and bought a piece of the field. As it turns out this just about fills the space between the road and the village. That has now gone to a developer with planning permission. I stand to make a considerable packet." Mogford looked somewhat shamefaced at having profited from the new road.

Luke burst out laughing. "He's got a bad conscience Ma'. Anyway I'm in favour, although it's a pity about the sheep, what about you Ma'?"

"I'm sure your Da' has weighed it all up," said Martha shortly. "I should think the value of the building land comes to more than the value of the other field; am I right Mogford?"

"Well, I wouldn't want us to lose by it," admitted Mogford.

"Anyway, I think it's great," said Luke. "The vicar will probably give thanks from the pulpit, perhaps even a sermon about Christian charity, more blessed to give than to receive . . ."

"Now about the hay and straw business," interrupted Mogford hastily. "I've rented barns here and there, and made some advance deals. How are you getting on with the lorry . . ."

Martha got up. "Don't forget we have a wedding to discuss when you can fit it in," was her parting shot.

A busy period followed. Winter wheat was being harvested up country. Luke and Tony made forays to collect straw. The Mogford rented barns were filling. Spare time was spent on the cricket ground. Cutting and rolling. A wicket to prepare. Local volunteer artisans were erecting a pavilion. It was a big improvement on the last ground. Clumps of elm trees on the perimeter offered shade. The vicar was euphoric. The village was in a fever of anticipation.

One evening a few weeks later, Martha and Mogford were visiting the ground to view progress. It looked smart. The grass had been fertilised and gang mowed and was a splendid green. Men in white overalls were painting the pavilion. The vicar was inspecting the wicket, and looking very pleased with himself. They watched as he faced up to an imaginary bowler and played a sweet shot, his eyes following the progress of the ball.

"Must have hit it to the boundary," smiled Mogford. "Otherwise we might have seen him run a single."

"Well, he's happy, you've made a lot of people happy, including me." Martha squeezed his arm. "It was a generous act, I'm very pleased with you."

Mogford looked uncomfortable. "Well I suppose a really good person would have chipped in the balance as well. I didn't exactly come out of the deal naked."

"A prudent good person, I'm even more proud of you," said Martha. "Anyway, it looks as though a deputation approaches."

The vicar had been joined by Blackie and a few

villagers. They approached and exchanged greetings. Then Blackie cleared his throat. "It be like this 'ere, Mr Mogford." Blackie paused to choose his words.

"For goodness sake get on with it," said the vicar irritably.

"Well it's like this 'ere," Blackie started again. "As our benefactor in the matter o' this 'ere pitch, us thought, this 'ere envelope . . ." he indicated a long brown official looking envelope in his hand.

The vicar clucked impatiently.

"It be a legal document, all fair an' proper, but there be a few small restrictions, which us felt ee wouldn't mind."

The vicar's patience snapped. "For goodness sake give him the envelope," he shrilled.

"No call to upset 'eersel' vicar, but 'ere be the document Mr Mogford, an' us gives ee our thanks, in a practical way." He handed over the envelope.

Mogford opened the envelope, his curiosity aroused. He and Martha read the document together. It gave Mogford sole grazing rights to the field for the next twenty years, subject to certain small restrictions. 'To be grazed by sheep only. Sheep to be removed two weeks before a match.' It was a superb gesture. Luke could have his sheep. Mogford was delighted. His obvious pleasure said more than his words. Everyone was smiling.

"Now do ee carry on strollin' wi' eer good lady Mr Mogford," suggested Blackie. "I could offer ee both a liddle celebration if ee were to stop by . . ."

"No Blackie, we'll just stroll, thanks all the same," said Mogford hastily, taking Martha's arm.

"It's so peaceful here," said Martha. They were under the trees and the evening was alive with birdsong; but Mogford was calculating.

"You know m'dear," he said. "If I were to purchase grazing for the twenty years, it would equal what I paid for the land. Of course at the end I don't have the land, or the grazing rights.

"You'll have your pension," comforted Martha.

Mogford ignored the interruption. "It's still a generous concession. The club could have made a lot of useful spending money from the grazing."

"Well you know what they say," said Martha. "What falls to the floor comes to the door."

"What falls to the floor . . . that's a bit obscure, isn't it m'dear. Whatever does it mean?"

Martha laughed. "I'm not too sure myself. I think it means, if you give something, you get something back. I'm sure I can think of a better one."

"No m'dear, it's all right. I get your meaning. It's certainly true in this case."

The next morning Martha was about to fry eggs. She turned to talk to Mogford, an egg in her hand. Luke entered suddenly with his usual gusto. Martha, startled, dropped the egg. It splattered on the floor. Luke placed a bucketful of eggs on the table.

He didn't understand his parents sometimes, what was so funny about dropping an egg.

"What falls to the floor comes to the door," chortled Mogford.

Luke sat down. His parents could behave in the most peculiar way sometimes. Still it was good to see them giggling and chortling. He had loftier things on his mind, like the cricket match, now looming close.

* * *

The day had started dull and overcast, but then the sun came out and touched the green sward with a lover's kiss, soft, and warm and unhurried.

The vicar had brought the weather into his prayers for the last two Sundays, and it looked now as though someone up there had taken heed.

The County players' coach was discreetly parked behind the pavilion, which sparkled with fresh paint. In the small fenced off enclosure in front, the players mingled; the great, the not so great, and the unknown.

Bob was there, chatting quietly; he had agreed to turn out on this auspicious occasion; he would open the batting with the vicar. Blackie, taking his cricket seriously, was judge-like in his sobriety. Luke and Betty were holding hands across the fence, heads close, talking. Tony, having earned his spurs during the season, was to come in at number five, after Constable Walters. The two of them were earnestly talking tactics, Tony paying heed to the advice given, his eyes only occasionally straying towards the Sedgemore family who were arranging deck chairs nearby. His glances were being returned. He was courting properly now, having had a rise in wages.

This and more was the scene which greeted Martha and Mogford, as they strolled arm in arm, well content with their village and the big occasion.

"Look Mogford, over there, isn't that Ben?"

And indeed it was Ben, complete with Barty and cart, entertaining a group of children with his conjuring tricks. The small cart held items for sale, clothes pegs, baskets, tin kettles and cutlery.

"I expect he sells the cutlery to people after he's ground theirs down to stilettos," said Mogford drily as they approached.

"Now, now," chided Martha. "We agreed that was on account of the cider."

Ben was delighted to see them. "Could pop down an' sharpen a few o' they ole knives later," he offered.

"No, no," said Mogford hurriedly. "The knives are fine, but do pop down. Stay over if you like. Are you back with your people now?"

"Only for weddings, funerals, and the like. All they young uns be gettin' motors. 'Tis not for the likes o' me an' liddle ole Barty 'ere. Us likes it as it is." He turned away as the children demanded his attention. "Us would like to stop the night if it be no trouble. Expect Barty 'ud like to meet up wi' your Daisy again."

The Mogfords strolled on. They could see the Percivals, complete with pony on the other side of the pitch.

"That little mare has found a good home," observed Martha.

"And it shows," said Mogford. "Young Clare has a good seat on a pony already; she's a real Percival. You know m'dear, folk like the Percivals don't have need of a pram, maybe not even a carrycot."

"Well I'm sure our Luke and Betty will have a pram and a carrycot." Martha was looking forward to the wedding, now only a month away. Sometimes she suffered a small pang of guilt in the pleasure she felt. The wedding was to be down here, in the village church. Things might have been a bit different if Betty's mother had been alive, and her father had been other than a lovable and woolly minded academic.

It wasn't as if she had organised it. Everyone had wanted it that way. She put her guilt away and gave herself to the pleasures of day dreaming; of carrycots, and prams and grandchildren.

Over by the refreshment tent, an alien group hovered. It was a knot of up country cattle market dealers. Mackay and his colleagues were not cricketers, but had decided to honour the occasion with their presence out of respect for Mogford. There was always the chance of discussing a bit of business with Mogford, and that young Luke was not far behind these days.

"You might have had a few sheep in the outfield for us to look at Mogford," grumbled Hamish Mackay.

"Haven't had sheep on for six weeks," said Mogford, shaking hands. "And it's been gang mowed every week. Can't have these County chaps running about in sheep dottles."

Mackay tipped his hat to Martha. "You look well Martha; that young rascal I sent you turned out all right?"

"Young Tony," laughed Martha. "Just look at him over there in his whites. He's one of the family now. Walking out with a very nice girl as well. I'm sure Hamish, it'll count heavily in your favour on the day of judgement. Anyway you're all invited to supper."

"There might be a few things to take into account on the other side," said Hamish doubtfully. "I can't afford to be on the side of the angels all the time. But we would all like to come to supper."

Many summer visitors had arrived for the occasion. Mrs May and her B & B friends were fully booked. It was rumoured that Mrs May had, with the upturn in business, returned to the fold, so to speak. She was again an active church worker, and it was believed that she had been in to clean up the vicarage, and cook the odd meal. She and her ladies were in charge of teas today, and there was every indication that an olive branch had passed between herself and the vicar.

The match was about to start. Luke had won the toss and elected to bat. Bob and the vicar were walking towards the wicket. Bob, still troubled by his knee, was limping slightly, and Tony was by his side to act as his runner.

"It's the vicar's big day," said Mogford. "Look how stiff and proud he carries himself."

They had a rear view from where they stood, and could only guess at the pride and pleasure on his face. A lifetime's ambition achieved.

Martha squeezed Mogford's arm. "Isn't it marvellous. So much has changed. This fine pitch, all those nice clean whites, a smart pavilion. The village folk are so much better off; we are better off; Luke about to be married; Tony growing up. This new road that we all worried about. It really all happened because of the road. Of course nothing ever stays the same, things are always changing."

The vicar turned to face the bowling. He was wearing one disreputable pad.

Mogford smiled. "It would appear not everything has changed, m'dear," he said.